T0149356

CAL COLE

Other books by Larry Layman

Tom Livengood

Paxton McAllister

Jesse Buxton

Tyler James

Buck Moline

Lema

Jose Baca

Brewster Daggit

Jon McKay

CAL COLE

L L Layman

iUniverse®

CAL COLE

iUniverse books may be ordered through booksellers or by contacting:

iUniverse
1663 Liberty Drive
Bloomington, IN 47403
www.iuniverse.com
1-800-Authors (1-800-288-4677)

ISBN: 978-1-5320-7948-1 (sc)
ISBN: 978-1-5320-7949-8 (e)

Library of Congress Control Number: 2019910882

Print information available on the last page.

iUniverse rev. date: 07/31/2019

Acknowledgements

In my by-gone years as a novel writing police officer I often gave thanks to the dregs, thieves, and crooks who stayed in and allowed me time to compose stories in my quiet warm comfortable parked squad car. Then I thanked the supervisors who looked the other way as I wrote these novels. But now, many years later, I have only my wife to thank for allowing me time to slip away to the shop and put pen to paper.

I have not written a story for several years, just busy with retirement and her honey-do's is all I can say. Getting back into my writing was not easy. Oh, the story was in my head and ready, the impetus to compose wasn't. I talked with a friend about getting started again. "The first word is always the hardest, the rest just flow." I said. She responded with, "Well, duh." Yesterday it snowed and I sat my desk pen in hand. I vacillated over that first word of the first sentence for an hour and the only thing that came to mind was "duh."

So, I wrote the word, "duh." The rest just flowed.

"Cal Cole," my tenth novel was done in record time. Then came life crisis after crisis. It took another six months to get it published, but it's done.

As I have not yet mastered word perfect, I want to thank Jennifer Phelps for turning my chicken scratches into typed words.

My cover artist and dear friend, Mike Goodale, passed away. My daughter, Mackenzie Clary stepped up to the plate and did my artwork.

And as always, I thank Tim Harper.

For my brother

Richard Layman

Chapter 1

▼

Duh day was still early but uncommonly hot, especially for an overcast sky. My chores at the barn were quickly finished. Then back at the cabin, I quietly washed off, better than usual, and changed into my Sunday best, that being my only white shirt which was much too big and a pair of trousers with only one patch over the knee. My hair I gave a quick brush, looked in the mirror and shrugged my shoulders. It was the best I could do. Breakfast was a wolfed-down hard-boiled egg and piece of bread.

Ever so tepidly I closed the cabin door behind me. The old man had never stopped snoring. I set off on the stone walled road to school, my only company was the constant cloud of mosquitos, something everyone in southeast New Hampshire endured or ignored. The first mile, the blood sucking bastards, as my father called them, were just a nuisance. As I walked the second mile, sweat began to bead on my face and the swarm became near intolerable. It was hard to believe that the beautiful piney forests could breed so many blood suckers. Harder still to believe I was their only source of sustenance.

Yet I continued, the school house was less than a half mile of swatting ahead.

Today was the last day of school for the year, maybe for the rest of my life, as I had completed all eight grades.

Behind me, still abed for sure, was my slumbering, snoring, father. He had given me instructions for the day, first chores then gardening. School graduation was not high on his list of priorities. A piece of paper was all I was to get this day. There was plenty of work at home, all mine, as his calling was much higher, the Lord's work. He had just tons of praying to do when he got up.

Waiting for me at school was my diploma, my golden bookmark, but most importantly, Jenny.

Jennifer Lynn Prescott had been my friend, or so I thought, for the three years I had spent in this school with her. Actually, secretly, she was the love of my life, though I had never once told her of my feelings. In fact, I rarely had even talked to her outside of the school setting.

Yesterday, she had asked me to help her carry her books home after graduation. I was elated, excited beyond words. Jenny had asked me to walk her home.

Two possibilities presented this day, one stay home and pull weeds or two, spend time with Jenny. The decision was easy.

This was going to be the greatest day of my life, all 13 years of it.

Jenny, like many of us in school, was a war baby. At the conclusion of the Civil War, the victorious Yankees marched home more than eager to start their families. Jenny's dad was no exception. Despite the loss of a few fingers he was able to resume, most successfully, his marital endeavors. Well he did too, as Jenny, his first born, was near perfect in all regards. She was just the prettiest girl in the school and probably the entire world. Jenny's mother had some input too as she was absolutely the most beautiful full-grown woman I had ever seen.

I was born several months ahead of Jenny, an only child, son of Horace Coleman, a traveling preacher. Three years ago, he had secured a small parsonage in Fitzwilliam, with it came our cabin and a few rock walled acres. Horace never fought in the war. His war efforts and contributions were those of comfort to the widows left behind. He constantly ministered to the bereaved, plenty there were. Dad had been too religious, big, fat, and long winded for the army. He hailed from Boston.

My late mother, Nadine, was from war torn Pennsylvania. She had fled the fighting with a sizable purse in hand. Most of her family had perished. She arrived in Boston only to be swept up in bereavemental comfort by my father. His degree of comfort was proportional to her purse. When the money was gone, so were they, moving frequently from church to church, county to county until he landed the Fitzwilliam parsonage. Mom died shortly thereafter.

Horace Coleman's silver tongue and litany of verse and prayer could not save my ailing mother. With her went my buffer from my father. Life with the Reverend Coleman was not pleasant.

My mother had, for the most part, home schooled me, first by teaching me to read the Bible then insisting I read literally everything in print. At the Rindge school, I was placed in the fifth grade because it was age appropriate.

Mrs. Anderson, the teacher, saw right off I was placed well below my grade level, but she worked with me separate from the others. I was allowed to read whatever I wanted and not be encumbered with the mundane rote others endured. School was an escape from my father, I loved it.

As I walked, swatted, and day dreamed of my pending walk with Jenny, I saw ahead Mrs. Anderson standing in front of the old stone church, which doubled as our school house. Several children were running about. Mrs. Anderson was a war widow for sure comforted by my father. She had been married into the Gordan family, her husband was killed at Gettysburg.

I hated the Gordan boys, all three of them. They were miscreants for lack of a better term. John, the oldest and biggest Gordan was 16, Ralph, his younger brother, was almost as tall but stocky of frame. Both were evil. Richie, their 15-year-old cousin who lived with them, was short, fat and mean; a sadistic kid. He loved to kill cats, puppies, and me if he could.

All three Gordan boys were in the sixth grade and had been for several years. I was sure their parents sent them to school for relief purposes, as they probably didn't like them either.

Mrs. Anderson coddled the trio as her job depended on her attempts to educate their feeble minds, but her control of the three was nil. They never did their assignments, talked back, and hooked whenever the mood struck.

Me, I was glad when they did. This day, most unfortunately for me, they had not hooked as all three stepped out into the road between me and the school house door. They were not looking at the school, they were glaring at me.

The mosquitoes were now the least of my concerns. I had just gone from swatter to swattee.

Chapter 2

―――――▼―――――

"Well looky here, boys. If it isn't sweet little Calvin Coleman," sneered John.

"The teacher's pet," added Ralph.

"Yea," was all Richie said, but his eyes were wild, and he was moving towards me, fists clenched.

"The smartest boy in the school," said Ralph, who was now on the move, just behind Richie.

"Thump him," ordered John.

With that Richie was coming at me like a raging bear. Richie was just an inch or two taller than me, but he had me by a hundred pounds. The others were men to me. I was five foot five and 100 pounds at best, and this was about to be my first fight ever.

Richie hit me on the fly and drove me to the ground. I landed flat on my back with the wind in my lungs expelled. Little could I do as Richie sat my chest smacking me with lefts and rights to the face.

I could hear him laughing, "Teacher's pet, teacher's pet."

The other two put their boots to me causing great pain.

It was Mrs. Anderson who saved the day, she and Jenny.

"Stop it," they screamed. "Stop it now!"

Mrs. Anderson dragged Richie off me. The other two backed off. Richie kept trying to return for the kill but my saviors held their ground standing between Richie and me. I had rolled over but had great difficulty getting up. Bent over like I was, I saw the ground covered red with blood, mine.

Now about every kid in the school had gathered about, all yelling at the

Gordans. I'm sure the Gordans could have whipped them all, but apparently there is power in numbers, as the Gordans walked off yelling insults and dares.

Me, I was battered good, but worse, I was sobbing. I had been beaten, bloodied, and now embarrassed. I was crying, and in front of Jenny and the whole school.

I was led into the school by Mrs. Anderson and Jenny, each had an arm. Once inside they got my nose to stop bleeding with cold compresses. I was cleaned up as best they could. My white shirt was covered with blood. It was removed and replaced with a shirt from someone, I knew not who. All in all, the better part of an hour was spent on my repairs, one eye was swollen near shut, the other was turning into a shiner. My nose had stopped bleeding and was apparently still centered. I knew I had bruising to my legs from being kicked, I chose not to mention those wounds for fear of losing my trousers in front of the ladies. No underwear did I own.

At 10 AM, as scheduled, the Graduation Ceremony began. Everyone moved places in the class room to the seats they would occupy next year. The eighth graders, the real graduates, moved to the front of the class to say their good byes, all six of us; me, Jenny, Elizabeth, Robert, Todd, and Brian.

Mrs. Anderson began, "We all want to congratulate the eighth graders. They will be moving on to their own endeavors. Each has successfully completed the curriculum. A round of applause please."

The seated students clapped their hands, but as I looked the room, all eyes were on me. I knew not what they were thinking, but I'm sure none would have traded places with me.

"And now for the special award I give every year, the golden bookmark. This award is given to the student who has read 50 books and completed 50 book reports, Calvin Coleman."

As she handed me the thin gold-plated piece of metal, she smiled, "I'm so proud of you Calvin." Then she whispered, "You could have taught the class."

She gave me a hug and a diploma, then did the same for the other five.

"It's a big world out there, you six go see it."

Simple as that it was over. We grabbed our stuff and walked out the door. I could see right off Jenny had no more than a small satchel to carry. She certainly didn't need a cry baby like me to carry it, but she flipped to me anyway.

"Walk me home, Calvin." she said.

And I did.

Jenny lived about a mile or so south of the school, down a rock fenced road just like the one I walked. Everything of value had a rock wall.

We walked and talked all the way. I wished she lived ten or 20 miles away, I so enjoyed the sound of her voice. Once beyond sight of the school, she reached down and held my hand. Right then I wished she lived a thousand miles away; I didn't want to ever let that hand go.

At the top of a rise, she dropped my hand and pointed to a clap board house surrounded, of course, by a rock wall.

"That's it, that's our house." she said not extending her hand back.

I was disappointed with both; our hand holding was over.

"Would you sit the porch with me? My mother has tea brewed for us, tea and some cookies."

"She knows I was coming?"

"Of course she does, I tell her everything."

Once on the porch she directed me to a two-person swing suspended from a porch rafter.

"Wait here, I'll get the tea."

Jenny returned with tea, cookies, and her parents.

"Oh my god, you poor boy. Those Gordan ruffians really did you in. Animals are what they are, animals!" said her mother. Her father said not a word, but he did take notice of my person. I felt like he was doing a different type of examination. I noticed the missing fingers along with part of his right hand.

Mrs. Prescott began an examination of my wounds.

"You should see a doctor; you are really hurt. Jenny said you were so brave." said the mother as she and the father left the porch, apparently satisfied I was not going to die in their swing. Right then I knew Jenny for a liar and thought all the more of her.

Jenny and I sat, talked, sipped, and ate for most of an hour. Finally, I excused myself and took my leave.

"I need to get home," I said. "Chores to do."

"When will I see you again?" she asked.

As I got up, she took my hand, leaned over and gave me a kiss.

"Soon," I smiled. I handed her my golden bookmark. "This is for you."

As I turned towards the road, I saw him coming, my father, the Reverend Coleman in his dilapidated buggy being pulled by Rita, our sway-backed, older-than-dirt mare.

"Over here boy," he bellowed.

Obediently, I walked towards the buggy as he was lumbering out, God he was a big man.

"Mrs. Anderson said I might find you here. Don't you have gardening to do?"

He said nothing about my injuries, he just busted me hard across my face with the flat of his hand, the force of which flattened me out again. Richie had hit hard, but he was just a piker compared to the Reverend. That slap could be heard clear up in Rindge.

I was now accustomed to being hit, tired of being embarrassed, and just plain mad, too mad to cry.

I got up and walked away, up into the wood where he could not and would not follow. I heard him yelling at me, but I did not look back. I just kept walking.

Chapter 3

▼

Once well back in the forest I cut a game trail that, for the most part, paralleled the rock walled road Jenny and I had walked. I kept to the trail and out of sight. For sure I was not going home, not today, not ever. Mrs. Anderson said it was a big world out there and for us to see it. I was going to do just that, just as soon as I was ready.

As I walked and thought, I began to formulate a plan. It wasn't much of one, but ideas were coming to mind.

First, one does not start out with only a borrowed shirt and a pair of single patched go-to-church trousers. Eating is important. Proper travelling attire is necessary. A means to provide for both is a must. I would need a job, build up some cash, and have a destination.

Other feelings had welled up inside of me this date. First was Jenny and how much I enjoyed her voice, her presence, and especially her touch. Secondly, there was rage. I had been soundly trounced by John, Ralph, and Richie Gordan and for no reason other than being different. I was definitely smarter and tried very hard in school, but I was also smaller and unaccustomed to fighting.

I was an easy victim. There had to be more, they could have beaten me up anytime they wanted for the past three years. Something had triggered them, something had changed.

"Jenny," I said aloud.

One of them, maybe all three had eyes for Jenny. Jenny must have told someone of her plans for the walk home after school and they got word. That had to be it, had to be.

My rage was not only the Gordans. The Reverend Coleman was there too. Oh, I had taken more than my share of whippings over the years, but never in front of anyone other than ma.

"Spare the rod, spoil the child," he would often quote.

Today he had crossed the line. I vowed he would never touch me again. I walked.

Once back near the school I was on my home turf. I knew all the back trails and lanes to our cabin. It wasn't long before I could see it. The buggy with Rita still harnessed was in front. I skirted our acreage and headed up the back trail to my diggins.

We moved here when I was ten. Like all boys I had explored. Way back, way, way, back in the timber I had found a mountain stream that led to a lake. Another brook flowed from that lake. I had made me a camp where the brook flowed out.

A great place it was. Over the years I had built a cabin of sorts and stocked it with provisions and means. It wasn't much to look at, in fact someone could look right at it and not seen it for what it was. They would just see big boulders and some dead fall.

The mystery was how these big stones even got here. There were three of them together leaning on one another. Inside was a dry room and natural vent for my fire. The dead fall was my only addition. I was able to close off the opening. Bear proof it was my thinking or prayer.

My diggins had a pallet with blankets for sleeping, some canned gods, dried beans and other essentials. I secretly always planned to leave home, but never considered when or how far to go. Most important in my hide out were my books, not the classics I read for school, I had all my dime novels hid here, my cowboy and western books, Kit Carson, Wyatt Earp, Wild Bill and others.

I had over 20 of them, all read over and over. If I had them at home the old man would have burnt them and beat me.

"The devil's work," he called them.

Devil be damned, I always told myself. More people were slain in his bible than in all the dime novels combined. And by God there was begetting going on. Lots of begetting with multiple partners. I guess there wasn't much else to do but kill and fornicate.

Here at my hide out there was plenty to do. I could read, fish, hunt, trap, and maybe even stab me a bear. I was always happy here.

Here I was safe from the Gordans, the Reverend, and everybody else, except the mosquitos.

Here I would stay, I just had a few things to do.

At first light I made a fire inside my hide out. I grabbed my knife from the kit I had stashed next to the pallet. It was but a short walk to the first brook pool below the lake discharge. I grabbed the line tied to a tree and pulled up my fish trap.

I could hear the flopping of fish. I must have had 20 perch of all sizes. From the trap I took the three largest, refastened the lid and gave it a heave back into the pool. Never had I not pulled up fish from that trap.

That knife was plenty sharp. All three fish were filleted in a minute. With the six filets rinsed, I went back to the fire, greased a pan and set it to the flame. Once it was hot, in went the perch. As they sizzled, I opened a jar of peaches.

"Aah, breakfast." I said to myself

When finished, I praised myself, "Good job, Cal, but you need salt."

I lazed about the rest of the day, reading my novels and planning. Tomorrow was Sunday and the Reverend would be at church. Tomorrow I would go back for my things. What I wanted most was my pistol and rifle, both gifts from Uncle Bob, my mother's brother. The old man never knew about them as I had them well hidden in the loft of the bar. The Reverend detested firearms.

"The devil's tools." he would say.

Right now, I was the devil himself and had need of my tools. After all, what good is a hide out if the outlaw in it isn't armed.

Chapter 4

▼

My plan was simple, wait until the Reverend went to church, slip in, gather what I wanted, then burn the cabin. That should teach him a thing or seven. Whacking me in front of Jenny was the last straw. Just how humiliated could one boy be.

I made my way to the cabin keeping off the path well into the wood. I wasn't going to leave a trace of passage.

When I could see the cabin I sat and waited, maybe an hour before I saw smoke from the cook stove. The old man finally emerged from the cabin, looked around, then made his morning trip to the privy. He then returned to the cabin. About a half hour later he came out in his Sunday preaching attire, retrieved Rita from the barn and hitched her to the buggy.

He sagged the rickety old buggy as his butt hit the seat. Then he flipped the whip on old Rita's rump and was off.

So far, so good.

I waited a while longer in case he returned. Once satisfied he was gone, I went on down to the cabin. I went in and got my things, both shirts, my work pants, and coat. From the cupboard shelf I took the half full flour sack, the tin of tea, and the sugar bag. All of these I put into the still partially full bag of dried beans.

"Salt." I uttered aloud.

I got the salt and a string of dried peppers and added them to the sack.

With the house raided, booty in hand, I went to the barn to retrieve my weapons.

Both guns, my Smith and Wesson model one revolver and Remington-Rider were hidden up in the hay loft back in the corner under the hay. They had been a gift from Uncle Bob on my tenth birthday. He had told me to learn how to use them and I would never go hungry. Ma had told me to hide them from the Reverend and never take them down if he was home. Three years I kept the faith and the weapons remained mine.

I dug out the guns and two remaining boxes of shells. As I started backing out from under the rafters, I heard the clomp of horses and voices.

"Well, this is it, Mr. Wisher," said a familiar voice, Elder John Miller, I was sure.

"Everything within the rock walls?"

"Yes, sir. Ours is not a wealthy parish, this is what we have to offer, a free place to live and half of the weekly offerings. Whatever you do between Sundays is your business."

"It's a small cabin, but the wife and I could make do. I see there is a garden started."

"It's yours," said the Elder.

"When will it be available?" asked Mr. Wisher.

"Tomorrow," answered the Elder. "We are going to discharge Coleman after today's service. We will not retain a man who beats his boy in public. After all, that kid of his is twice the man Coleman is. The boy was always quiet and studious. Mrs. Anderson over in Rindge swore by him. Once Mrs. Prescott made her report as to the slap down, Coleman' religious contributions are no longer needed. He's gone."

"Where's the boy?" asked the man.

"He was last seen going into the wood and not since."

"Run off, did he?"

"We only hope. He wasn't in the buggy and he don't seem to be here. Who knows?"

"I'll take the position and the place. You said it will be available tomorrow."

"I guarantee it. Coleman's choices are but two, vacate or go to jail."

The two edged off toward the house. I held fast in the loft, but moved over to a crack in the siding where I could see them dismount and go into the cabin. After less than a minute, they came out, shook hands, mounted their horses, and rode off.

"Damn," I said to no one.

I had wanted to burn down the cabin, but now I couldn't as another family had need of it. I had my hopes of being a real outlaw living in my hide out.

I was actually disappointed.

I grabbed up my weapons and shells. I returned to the house, grabbed a few more utensils and the tea pot, all of which fit into the bean bag, and headed back to camp.

I was truly, truly disheartened. An outlaw needed a reason to go on the run. So far, I had none.

Then I thought of the Gordans. I felt myself smirking, plan two.

Chapter 5

▼

Life at camp fell into what I considered an enjoyable routine, no real work was there to do, just things I wanted to do. I could sleep late, swim, fish, read my dime novels over and over, or hunt, all things pleasurable.

Hunting expanded my diet. I liked fish, but I really liked squirrel, or any other critter that I sighted in on.

My rifle, from Uncle Bob, was a Remington-Rider. It was a breech-loading, single-shot 22 cal. I could bark a squirrel at 40 yards with no problem. All I had to do was find one, aim just below his head and squeeze the trigger. Somehow, I had figured out that squirrels, upon hearing the crack of the rifle, immediately dropped their heads, generally the last sound they ever heard.

It was three years ago, just before Mom died that Uncle Bob had visited. My mother, Nadine, had not been a happy woman. Mostly she was dull eyed, slow of motion and prone to long periods of silence. She often stared at nothing, while she did nothing.

Two times I had noticed a change in her, once when I was five, the last was when I was ten. Both times Uncle Bob was visiting, both times the Reverend was away. Both times my mother was a different woman. She was happy and laughing. She was alive.

It was on the last visit that Uncle Bob gave me the weapons.

"Learn to shoot that rifle and you'll never go hungry" he said.

"Learn to shoot the revolver and you'll fear no one." was the second piece of advice.

Of course, he added my favorite dime novel quote, "God made man, Sam Colt made them equal."

His words of wisdom I adhered to as I had practiced long hours with each, my mother furnishing me boxes of bullets with the Reverend totally unaware.

"I'm going West," he told my mother and I. "You are welcome to come along. I want you to come. Arizona, I think. I hear there's land for the taking. They say God made a special place for his believers just under the Mogollan Rim."

"Calvin," my mother interjected, "would you go down to the well and get us a pitcher of water?"

I knew what that meant, leave, and I did.

About a half hour later, Uncle Bob came down to the well and gave me a big hug. He was a strong, rugged man, my idol I guess, but I could see he had been crying.

"Hard to leave you and our ma, but the west is calling my name. Take care of her. She's just damn special to me, you too. You will hear from me again."

I watched as he and that buckskin horse of his disappear and he was gone.

Mom was crying. She didn't care if I saw her either. She sobbed and sobbed. Three weeks later, she was dead.

It was a sad story I relived over and over. My reading was generally a diversion but short-lived at best. Jenny was an added burden. Only a week on the run now and I missed her too. Strange, I thought, how someone could miss something they never had. I missed her smile, her voice.

In fact, I missed any voice. Being an outlaw on the run was kind of lonely. That afternoon I shot a stupid partridge in a pine tree. Eat well I did.

My breakfast the next day was smoky, chewy left-over partridge. Not great, but satisfying.

I'd thought a good part of the night about Jenny, mom, and Uncle Bob. Realizing how lonely I was. I needed to hear a voice other than my own.

Our cabin was less than a mile's walk. With my revolver in my pocket and my rifle in hand, I headed to it. I wanted to see if the Reverend had vacated.

The cabin, much to my disappointment, was still there. Smoke came from the stack. I could smell bacon. I sat low and waited, watching. Soon a man came out, it was the new Reverend Wisher. He hitched a mule to a buckboard wagon and drove it west toward Fitzwilliam. After a while a pretty lady came out and walked to the garden. She was striking in all regards, just beautiful and she wasn't that old. I guessed her in her late teens. She began to hoe.

I walked down to the garden and got about ten feet away, totally undetected.

"Those are peppers in that row." I said.

The lady was obviously startled.

"Who are you, where did you come from?"

"Calvin Coleman ma'am, I used to live here. Those are peppers in that row, the next one is tomatoes."

"Calvin," she said.

"Yes, ma'am, Calvin Coleman—and those over there are melons. I planted them but the one's last year were eaten by the bears. You'll need a dog if you want melon."

"Calvin you say." Still trying to recover. Then she asked, "Have you eaten today?"

"Burnt partridge." I replied.

"Well, set that rifle aside and come with me, you'll need more to eat than that if you are going to hoe this garden.

Nice, nice lady. Bacon, eggs, potatoes and coffee, nice lady.

Her name was Mell, short for Melba. She was a talker. She gave me the rundown of the past eight or nine days. Most of the story came as we hoed, the rest as I split firewood.

Reverend Coleman had been discharged from the parish for lack of character. He had beaten his son in public and had made unwanted advances to Mrs. Anderson. He left the church mad, shouting, threats and obscenities, calling them all blood-sucking bastards.

I knew we were talking about the same man.

The Reverend Coleman had vacated the farm that very day taking only his clothing and a few whatnots. He was now on the run because he took old Rita and the buggy, which belonged to the church.

"People wondered if he had killed you," said Mell. "I'll have to report you are alive and well. We would not want him hung for murder."

"I guess not." was all I said.

I went to stacking the stove wood.

"That's not all," she said. "Two days after your incident at the Prescott's those three Gordan boys showed up there. They assaulted Jenny in just the worse way possible then ran off laughing. Her father took off after them with his rifle but lost sight. He went to their house and confronted their parents.

Orville Gordan went after Prescott and got himself shot for his efforts. He died right there, in the front yard."

"Jenny," I asked, "Is she okay?"

"We don't know. When the sheriff went to talk to Prescott the place was abandoned. The Prescotts just up and moved."

"Where?"

"No one knows, they are just gone."

"What happened to the Gordan boys?"

"They are on the run."

There was a lot to digest here, a lot. I needed to think. I picked up my rifle and headed back towards my hide out.

"Come back anytime," yelled Mell. "It's your garden as much as ours. You come back now."

Some outlaw I was. The Reverend, the Gordans, and the Prescotts were all on the run. I had the hide out and was the one who didn't need to hide.

Chapter 6

━━━━━━━━━━▼━━━━━━━━━━

The more I thought about it the madder I got. I wasn't sure what abused in the worst way was, but I had a good idea. If the Prescott's had fled because her father had shot their father, would there ever be justice served. I wondered if the Gordans even knew.

When I got to my lake I saw a goose sitting hear the shore line. I ducked low and worked my way up towards the bird using all the cover there was. I was close. There was a tree to brace my rifle on and I used it, took aim and removed a goose head. Much to my chagrin, that dead goose flailed himself farther out into the lake. I was in no mood for a swim, but I got one in.

I'd never done it, but with effort I was able to skin the goose. The meat I filleted off the carcass in thin strips. Then I slowly jerked the meat over my cook fire.

While the meat dried, I fashioned myself a holster for my revolver and sheath for my knife out of a piece of hide that was stashed in the hide out. Then I cut myself a long strip for a belt. Once everything was cut, I soaked the hide pieces in a pot of boiling water until soft.

When pliable, I folded the sheath on my knife to form and sewed the two halves together. I cut a belt slot in the top. Then I did the same for the revolver. To hook the belt, I made a thong tie until I could find a proper belt hook.

By the time I finished it was dark. My repast was goose jerky that needed more salt and hot tea. I was good to go, or at least I thought so.

Dawn came late as I had to wait for it. Some more goose jerky and hot tea was breakfast. Then with my revolver loaded and holstered on the ride side of the belt, my sheathed knife on the other, rifle in hand, shells in my pocket, a blanket roll filled with jerked goose over my shoulder, I headed out. I wasn't quite the plainsman, but it would do.

I was going on the hunt.

It was more than a morning's walk to the Gordan's stead up by Monadack, especially when I kept well off the road, well out of sight.

When I saw their cabin, I eased up low to the ground to a place that offered adequate cover. Here I spent the rest of the day. People came and went, there was considerable activity but I did not see the trio I sought.

After dark the lights were doused and the house went dark. About an hour later I heard some rustling off in the wood to my right. Initially I thought it deer or maybe a bear, but a short time later, I saw three figures move from the wood to the house. There was a clear sky, stars and a moon. It was them; John, Ralph, and Richie. Richie, I recognized, even from a distance in the dark; short and fat.

They rapped the door a few times and it opened. Once inside the door was shut. The house was still dark except for just the faintest glow of a candle.

About an hour later, the candle light went out, the door opened, and the trio retraced their path into the wood. Again, I heard their rustling as they passed by me.

I had a place to start my hunt in the morning. For now, all I could do was eat and rest. The blanket roll was untied and I retrieved the jerky, chewed a bunch, then curled up in the blanket and slept.

At first light I was on the hunt. Their passage had been on a well-worn path that lead south-westerly through the pine. Slowly I moved along the trace carefully watching for tracks departing left or right. None did.

I was somewhat familiar with the area concluding that they must be heading to what I called Sandy Lake. There was a beach there, where older kids sometimes gathered to swim. They called it Bare Ass Beach.

On the north side of Sandy Lake, I knew there to be an abandoned cabin. My guess was I would find them there, and I did.

As they sat the porch, I sat my post. We waited. I knew what I wanted to do. I wanted revenge, for me and for Jenny. I knew I was going to shoot all three. I also knew my rifle would only hurt them. The chances of killing a full-grown man with my peashooter was next to nil, but hurt them it would.

I had time, what I needed was the right moment and the right target.

The day grew hot. About noon they picked up and walked around the lake to the beach. There they stared a bon fire. I eased around and found another spot to watch.

A girl appeared from the woods. She was alone, but I could see she was expected. I recognized her as their cousin, Amelia. She was 16 or 17, one of the girls who never went to school. All four stood the fire talking and laughing.

Then all four chucked off all their clothes and walked to the water's edge, still laughing. The boys I paid no never mind, but Amelia did have my undivided attention. She was a full-grown woman in all regards and with all the attributes. She wasn't pretty of face, but God almighty she was well endowed.

I doubt if swimming was the ultimate goal of the Gordans but out into the lake they all went, just laughing and cavorting. They were on that girl like stink on crap and she didn't mind a bit.

We were all distracted, but finally my purpose overrode my distraction. I slipped up to their bon fire, grabbed all their clothes and piled them on the fire.

Their focus being what it was, I just walked back into the timber totally unnoticed. I was less than 40 yards from the fire and well hidden, with my rifle in hand and four extra rounds in the other, I waited.

By and by, all four returned to the fire only to find their clothes still smoldering. God, almighty, you never heard such yelling and swearing.

I took careful aim and popped John right in the butt. They were confused as John screamed out in pain as the others didn't run. I reloaded, aimed and shot Ralph in his bare butt. Ralph went down screaming. That left Richie, who was on the run. He was farther away but his butt was bigger. I let him have one too. Down he went, yelling with pain. I reloaded, looked Amelia over as well as time permitted and smiled, she did not need shot.

I took one last look I had at the Gordan boys. All three were up and running away with bloody butts.

I'd done enough for today. I slipped away.

Now I was finally a real outlaw and glad I was.

Chapter 7

▼

I outlawed around the hide out for the next three days, mostly doing outlaw stuff; sleeping in, fishing, hunting, and cooking great meals on the old camp fire. I chuckled over and over about the shot butt Gordans, but when I thought of them, I kept seeing Amelia. Slut puppy she might well be, but she stirred feelings I did not know existed. She had a body that was rocking my world.

Once again, I needed to talk to someone, I needed to hear a voice, it was time to hoe a garden.

Like my previous visit to the farm, I waited until Reverend Wisher had hitched his mule and left before I approached. My holster and rifle were set inside the barn and I grabbed the hoe. By the time Mell came out I was almost finished.

"Well look who is here." she said, "Glad you came by. Hungry I suspect."

"Yes, ma'am."

"I'll make you a plate and don't you leave. I've plenty for you to do today."

By the time she returned, I had the stove wood for tomorrow split and stacked on the porch.

"Sit here, Cal," she said pointing to the porch step. "I'll be right back with your coffee."

I was a tea drinker, but was really appreciative of her coffee. I made a mental note to buy some if I ever got any money. I'd almost come to the conclusion, what good is outlawing if you had no money, nor a place to spend it if you did. More importantly, hiding out in the woods was not what it was cracked up to be, there was no one to talk to. The sound of a female voice was ever so pleasant.

"Here's your coffee, Cal," reaffirming my last thought.

She sat next to me.

"When you are finished, would you help me muck out the stalls? We need to put manure around some of the vegetables. It will help with the weeds and give some needed nutrition to the soil."

"Yes ma'am. I'll get right at it."

"Not until you've finished eating."

She was right about that. On the plate were eggs, a slice of ham, potatoes, and a big dollop of oatmeal covered in sugar. It was great and I ate with gusto.

"I believe you have a story to tell me Calvin."

"What about?"

"You know."

"What?"

"Listen here young man, you just can't go around shooting people."

"Me?"

"Yes, you. First the Reverend came home all excited, half laughing, talking about the Gordan shooting. He said someone shot all three of them in the buttocks then set them off into the wood buck naked. The boys were spotted limping along the Jaffery road, their butt and legs covered in blood. The sheriff was called and took them into custody. As none of the boys could sit down due to their wounds, they elected to stand the back of wagon as he drove them over to the doctor's in Peterborough. The whole county saw it and roared with laughter."

She paused, "And what do you have to say about it?"

"What?" I answered as I dug into the oatmeal.

"The shooting, silly."

"I guess those Gordans needed shot." I answered.

"That is the same thing the sheriff said when he was here looking for you."

"Here?"

"Yes, he was here yesterday and asked if I had seen you. I didn't lie, I said that I had and you often did work for me in exchange for meals. He asked me when you were last here. I told him you were here gardening for me every day for the past week."

"You did?"

"Yes, I did, but you need to promise me that you won't go around shooting folks just because they need it."

Well, she had lied for me so I did too.

"No ma'am, I won't."

"The sheriff said when he left that the Gordan boys needed shot if anyone ever did and that he was closing out his investigation as shooter unknown. Besides, he said that the Gordans moved, lock stock and barrel headed for parts unknown. He had no complainant. The case was closed."

"Closed?"

"Yes, Calvin, no one is looking for you. You no longer have to live back in the woods. I talked to my husband, you are welcome to live here."

"No, ma'am, thank you, but you are right. I love the woods but I need to get on with my life. I'm 13 you know, and able to work and support myself."

"Thirteen you say."

"Yes, but getting on towards 14," I answered.

"A job around people will do you well. Let's start here. Get mucking out the barn, pay is 10 cents an hour starting right now."

I made my first 55 cents.

Chapter 8

The next morning, I hit the road in search of employment. I had 55 cents and wanted more. As I passed our old farm, I knocked on the door. Mell answered still in her night gown. She was a looker, no doubt about it. Reverend Wisher was a lucky man.

"I just wanted to thank you and say good-bye."

"Will you come in for something to eat?"

"No, ma'am, I ate up all I had left. I'm good."

"Will you come back?"

"Only if I need a friend or a hide out. Thank you so much for your kindness. You are a wonderful lady."

She reached out and gave me a big hug. As she did, I saw more than I needed to.

Embarrassed I was, but I hugged her back and accepted just the nicest kiss on the cheek. I backed away, making sure to keep eye contact, hard though it was. What I had seen, could not be unseen. What I had seen would always be remembered.

"Good-bye, Mell." I said backing away.

My searching eyes looked for the road and found it. I put my best foot forward. I was off to see Mrs. Anderson's big world out there.

I had my gun belt and holster secreted away under my shirt; the revolver was easy to hand. The rifle was hidden within my blanket roll along with my few traveling possessions. Both ends of the blanket roll were roped shut. The rope hung from my shoulder.

In Jaffrey, I found no work, but a man told me they were always looking for help at the mill in Peterborough.

Late afternoon I walked in the mill office. There was a big burley man at the desk. His arms were huge. He might have been the strongest man I have ever seen.

"I'm looking for work, sir."

He looked me over and smiled.

"You won't find employment here, boy. You aren't big enough to pull your own weight. Sorry, but come back when you grow up."

"I'm 14," I lied.

"Like I said, come back when you have some beef on your bones."

"Well, thank you anyway." I said. As I started to leave, he said," Hey, kid. Go across the bridge, third building on the right. That's Martha's Eatery. She told me at breakfaster her swamper had drug up. She needs help. Tell her Big Ben sent you."

"Thank you, sir."

"Come back when you have grown, boy."

Martha's Eatery wasn't much, just a long bench with a mis-match of chairs down each side. There was a woman at the rear tending something over a big cook stove. She was middle aged, short and heavy. Her apron was grease stained, her hair unkept.

"We will not be open until four pm." she yelled, "Come back then if you want a meal."

"Yes, I'd love a meal, but what I need is a job."

"A bit young, aren't you?"

"Fourteen," I lied again.

"On the run, are you?"

"No, I walked here."

The lady smiled, "Walked you say. Where from?"

"From the mill, Big Ben said he couldn't use me, but you have need of a swamper."

"Ever swamped before?"

"No."

"Ever had a job before?"

"Yes." I kind of lied. I had been employed for a total of five and a half hours the previous day.

"Who did you work for?"

"I was a farm hand for Melba Wisher."

"Mell Wisher that's married to Reverend Wisher?"

"Yes, ma'am."

"Did she give you a letter?"

"No."

"Your reason for leaving?"

"I'm going on the road, ma'am. Mrs. Anderson told me to see the world. This is my first stop."

"Mrs. Anderson, the school teacher down in the Rindge?"

"Yes, ma'am."

"Your name, boy."

"Calvin Coleman."

"Well, I'll be. I've heard of you from Mrs. Anderson. She said you were a good lad. She called you the reader."

She pointed to a line of pegs along the wall.

"Tie on that apron over there on the peg. I pay ten cents an hour and a meal. I have two shifts. Be here at six am and work until nine am. Be back at four pm and work until close. That's generally 50 cents a day and two meals. I deduct for second helpings and dessert. No work on Sundays."

I hung my blanket roll on the peg where the apron was and tied the apron around me.

Her kitchen was a mess.

"Start there with those breakfast dishes, we will need them in 30 minutes."

Simple as that, I had a job and was up to my elbows in dirty dishes. What was better, I was going to fill my belly too.

The work came easy to me as I had years of experience in the kitchen with my mother. This was a bigger kitchen was the only difference. I kept busy and generally had things done before I was directed to. I waited tables, carried meals and plates back and forth, keeping the water glasses full.

Several customers left a penny on their plate. I asked Martha about it. She said it was a tip for good service and I could keep them.

The first hour I had five cents. I got another four cents the second hour. As the last customer left, I had all dishes washed and stacked, pots and pans clean and hanging, the kitchen floor swept.

While Martha was counting her till, I washed off the long table and swept the dining floor, then straightened the chairs.

"Nice job young man, but you forgot to eat. Your meal is warm on the stove. Eat up. Calvin, can you do this every shift, every day?"

"I guess, this was new to me."

"I have never seen a man work so steady with no waste of motion before. Who taught you how to do this?"

"My mother."

"She did well. I'm going to give you a pay raise on your first day. You can have 11 cents per hour, a meal, and your tips. Be here at six tomorrow morning."

I left with my belly full and an additional sixty-four cents in my pocket. I was one day on the road and rich. I had one dollar and nineteen cents cash money.

Tomorrow I would be even richer. Maybe my outlaw days were behind me.

Chapter 9

▼

The next morning, I arrived early, no idea what time it was as I had no time piece. The previous night was fitful. I had picked a pretty spot along the mill stream, but found the ground hard and the blood suckers ravenous.

The door was unlocked. I went in, Martha had not yet arrived. With nothing else to do, I grabbed my apron from the peg and replaced it with my blanket roll, and went to work.

I fired up the cook stove and set both the filled tea pot and coffee pot on top. I added tea to one, coffee to the other, the amount was just a guess.

She had a slab of bacon in what she called the cold chest. I found her cutting board and went to slicing strips. I was so occupied when she came in the door.

"Calvin, you are early."

"I had no clock, besides I had nothing else to do."

"Where are you staying?" She asked.

"I found a nice spot along the mill stream."

"My Lord! Shame on me. I should have asked. A young man on the road would not have a place. Shame on me! If I would have known I would have taken you home."

"I'm okay ma'am, I've slept out many a night."

"We will see about that." She said.

Then it was back to business. She went to cooking and I to swamping. The customers came in and took their accustomed chairs. They would be greeted by Martha.

"Morning, Ben."

"Morning, Martha."

"The usual?"

"The usual."

"Morning, Henry."

"Morning, Martha."

"The usual?"

"The usual."

For two hours nothing changed. Martha greeted and cooked, I swamped. She did change the routine with one man. She had called him, O'Phalon, an older, tall, skinny fellow with glasses. She went and sat with him a while and talked. Both would glance at me as they did. I could not hear their conversation. I kept working as it was none of my business, though their glances unnerved me a tad as I was apparently the subject of conversation.

The breakfast crowd vacated leaving me 12 cents in tip money. I just could not believe their generosity. I had one dollar and thirty-one cents pocketed now with a chance to make more in the afternoon.

When I finished up my duties, Martha told me to join her at the table.

"Your breakfast is hot on the stove, bring it and two cups of coffee."

"Yes, ma'am." I said, complying.

Once seated, Martha said, "Do you remember Mr. O'Phalon, the man I was talking to?"

"Yes, ma'am."

"O'Phalon runs our local post office, that and a freight business. His place is across the street."

"Yes, ma'am, I noticed the sign."

"O'Phalon has two things of note. One is a part-time job for a young man, sort of like you do here. Just odds and ends, some mail sorting, just whatever. It's not a government job, like his, but it's a foot in the door. The hours just happen to be 9 AM until 4 PM."

She was smiling.

"And he pays the going rate of 10 cents an hour. He is interested in you."

"He is?"

"Yes, but there is a stipulation."

"What?" I asked, although it didn't matter, I was excited.

"You can't quit here. I have never had such a competent help."

"Thank you."

"Secondly, and most important to me, he has a spare room on the backside of his building that you can use. You will not be sleeping on the ground anymore."

"Wow!"

"Now go and see O'Phalon, he's expecting you."

I washed my dishes, put them away, hung up my apron, shouldered my bed roll and walked across the street.

The sign said, "Postal Service and Freight." The building was a big log structure. One story, but tall with a covered front porch for loading wagons. A wagon was in the process of being loaded. It was positioned parallel to the porch, its team of mules hitched and resting, their heads down and tails switching the occasional fly.

As I entered, I saw O'Phalon and another man talking.

"Calvin," O'Phalon said, "glad you are here. Put that stack of boxes in the back of that wagon out front."

I had a job and I went right to it. When I had the wagon loaded, the man came out, looked over his load, climbed the seat and flipped his mules.

"Yup, yup!" He ordered and he was moving. "Nice job kid, thanks!"

I went back inside and O'Phalon showed me around.

"Your job is basically to do as directed and then whatever you see needs done. Pretty simple. Martha said you can read."

"Yes, sir."

"Good, you can help me sort mail. You can count?"

"Yes, sir."

"Good, I'll show you how to sell stamps and freight loads."

"Yes, sir."

"Follow me," he said.

O'Phalon led me to the rear of the building and opened a door. "Here is where you can stay."

The room was almost as big as our cabin. There were boxes stored throughout, but also a bed and table with a lamp. The room had its own exit door. It was like an enclosed back porch.

"The privy is out that door," he said.

"Martha said you were industrious and honest. Those are the most important attributes an employee can have."

"Yes, sir."

"She also said that you are a good shot."

"She what?"

"We will not discuss the matter again." He said. "I had no use for them boys either. You are now my what-not man and night watchman. I hope you can use that pistol under your shirt as well as the rifle in your blanket roll."

"Yes, sir." Was all I said.

"I pay on Saturday, 10 cents an hour. We work six days. Sundays, I go to church. The broom is by the front door."

My blanket roll I tossed to the bed. I found the broom and went to work.

"Two jobs, a roof over my head, plenty to eat, money in my pocket, more money to come. What more could I ask for my second day on the road?" I told myself. "And all I had to do was work hard. Or maybe just shoot someone who needed shot."

I wasn't sure which. I didn't care. It was raining.

Chapter 10

▼

Two winters had come and gone; spring was the season. Trees were in bud and the grass had turned green. The rains fell but I was warm, dry, fed and still piling up my money. There was well over six-hundred dollars, all coin, in the floor boards under my bed.

My life was a routine. Mornings with Martha, then five hours at the freight house, evenings back at the restaurant, with Sundays to my own devices.

Those idle Sundays became my delight. I could hunt, fish, read or visit. Squirrels were my favorite wild game of choice with an occasional rabbit, grouse, or turkey. Rare was the time I missed with my rifle. Often times I would hit them with my pistol just for practice. Martha would buy whatever I shot and serve it to her customers on Monday. If I bored with hunting, I would fish, pole and line, or just pull my basket traps, it didn't matter. Martha would buy them too. If I brought her fish, she served fish on Monday. She didn't pay much, but the money offset my ammunition purchases.

Some Sundays I chose to read, especially if there was snow on the ground. There was a lady in town, Mrs. Eagleton, who had her own private library. She allowed me to read anything she had in exchange for grouse or turkey. I shot for her too.

Mrs. Eagleton's collections were generally classics or non-fiction. What I still preferred were the dime novel westerns, many of which I intercepted in my postal duties. Never did I steal one, but read them I did. I'd open the envelop, read, reseal, and then include it in the next day delivery, the recipient none the wiser.

Stories of the wild west still excited me, almost as much as those images of Amelia and Mell, which I could not forget.

Amelia, I had seen once since, in passage as I walked the road to Rindge. She was with another girl walking the opposite direction. They paid me no never mind as far as I knew.

I said, "Hello." As we passed. They responded in kind. She was totally dressed, but I sure didn't see her that way.

Mell on the other hand, was my most common destination. I would visit the Wishers on a regular basis, maybe every other month as it was quite a walk. Nice lady she was, and my best friend.

Over the past two winters something else was happening to me. At first, I thought my clothes were shrinking and my boots were defective as I was constantly at the second-hand store looking for bigger sizes. Then one day, as I was talking to Martha, I noticed I was looking down at her.

I was still growing.

When I stood on the scales at the freight house, I was forced to keep moving the counter weights, clear up to 166 pounds.

Big Ben had even asked me if I was interested in mill work yet.

"No, sir." I replied. "My allegiance is still to Martha and O'Phalon."

"Well, see me when you are ready, Cal Cole. I could use a good man like you."

Cal Cole was now what I was called. It started as a nickname by who, I didn't remember. Just a restaurant customer called me Cal Cole and it just stuck. Everyone began calling me the same.

I didn't mind, Calvin was sort of dorky and I had no desire to be a Coleman. Not an ounce of respect did I have for Reverend Coleman, nor any desire to see him again.

Cal Cole was good with me. I liked it so much I carved it into the stock of my rifle and grip of my pistol, which I still wore under my shirt. The only other change I had made was a real leather belt and gun holster with loops for my small caliber rounds, and a sheath for my knife. It was the same set up that I saw on the cover of many a dime novel.

Besides, Uncle Bob had said that a man who wore a pistol was in fear of no other. I walked where I chose, generally from Martha's Eatery to the Postal Services and Freight and back again.

My employment tasks at the Postal Service and Freight or PS&F had expanded greatly. Oh, I still swept and loaded wagons but most of my time was spent sorting post or dealing with freight and customers. Within a few months I had the business down pat. O'Phalon would even take days off and leave the business to me. Few, if any, were my mistakes.

As to my night watchman duties, I had no problems. It was a small town and even though there was never a word mentioned to me, everyone probably knew that any attempt at burglary or robbery might result in a bullet in the butt or worse.

My life was a comfortable routine. In Peterborough I might be, but someday I was going west.

Horace Greely had written, "Go west young man, go west." I still intended to, but right now I had dishes to finish.

"Martha," I called out, "I'm finished. I'll see you at four."

"Okay, check with today's post. I'm expecting a package. If it is there, will you bring it back with you?"

"Yes, ma'am." I said, closing the door behind me.

There was a different wagon at the rail, not anyone I knew.

As I stepped up to the porch, I could hear arguing inside. O'Phalon was having trouble with someone. I opened the door and slipped in.

"Get out, God damn you, get out!" ordered O'Phalon.

"Why you, old man, you can't talk to me that way!" yelled a stranger. He was 30ish, tall and broad with a full beard, dressed like a farmer.

Crack was the sound as the stranger smacked O'Phalon across the face with his right hand. I saw the blood fly.

No thought did I have as to my weapon under my shirt, still easy to hand, no time to react other than grab the man from behind and pull him back. He pulled free but I popped him good dead in the mouth with my fist, then once more with the other hand. Neither contact had seemed to have had much effect as the man pounded me hard with his fists blow after blow. Knocked senseless I was. My last memory was his boot coming toward my head.

Chapter 11

▼

I could hear excited voices everywhere over the ringing in my ears.

"What happened?"

"Who did it?"

"Get the doctor!"

"Somebody, ride for the sheriff!"

There was either an echo or everybody was saying the same thing.

Martha was bent over me, "You'll be okay, Cal, you are going to be fine." She was lying for sure.

I hurt to the bone, all of them, and I couldn't see, not much anyway.

"Rest now, the doctor will be here." she said.

Wasn't much else I could do; I was commanding my body to get up but it didn't respond. God, I hurt.

With my head turned slightly, I could see O'Phalon on the floor next to me. He was moving, he was alive, I just wasn't sure about me.

Eventually, I was assisted to my feet, O'Phalon was already up, telling his story to 10, maybe 12 people crowded into the freight office.

I wasn't sure what he was saying as I was helped to my bed in the rear; Martha on one side, Big Ben on the other. Once abed, Big Ben lied and said I would be alright. He left me to the care of Martha, who somewhere found hot water and a rag, which she used to clean me up. From the color of the rag, I knew I had been bleeding aplenty.

The doctor came, looked me over, pulled from his bag a needle and thread. He began sewing up an apparent hole in my head. Hurt like I was, his little poking and pricks were but a nuisance. When he was done, I saw him smile as he examined his work.

Then he poured some sort of ointment over the wound that hurt like hell. I was bandaged and he left telling Martha to just let me rest. That there were no broken bones as far as he could tell.

"When will he be able to come to work?" she asked. "I can't run that damn restaurant without him."

"Maybe tomorrow, maybe. We will see."

"Now Cal," she said, "You rest, doctor's orders."

As she sat the bed, I did as directed. Sleep was an escape from the pain.

Later in the day, the sheriff came, woke me up and asked me some questions. Mush mouthed as I was, I did my best to answer.

"Name?" he asked.

"Cal Cole," I responded.

"Oh ya, Cal Cole it is now and don't blame you a bit. Okay Cal Cole, what happened?"

I told the sheriff exactly what happened, as it happened.

"Did you know the man?" he asked.

"No."

"Have you ever shot him before?" with the emphasis on him.

"No sir, not yet." I replied.

"Well, don't. You would be my first suspect and I don't need any more incidents involving Mr. Cal Cole. Do you understand me? Let the law do its job."

"Yes, sir." I lied.

Later that night O'Phalon came into my room. Martha was with him. He lit the light and sat the chair.

"Get up, Cal. Skootch your butt over to the table. I've hot tea and dinner for you."

I did as directed and was surprised at my abilities, but I still hurt just everywhere.

"Now sip some tea and eat."

"You need your strength, boy. We need you to recover. We flat need you. Both our businesses need you up and moving. We have come to rely on you."

"Yes, we have," added Martha. "Now eat."

As I sipped and munched, O'Phalon told his story.

"His name was Derek Garrison. He lives up north in Greenville. We deliver to him from time to time.

I remembered the name and address.

"He had horse harness ordered from who knows where and it was to have been delivered several weeks ago. He came in demanding his harness which we had not yet received, and I told him so. He accused me of stealing his shipment. I told him over and over we did not have it, that we knew nothing about it. Called me a liar and thief over and over. Finally, I told him to get out. He went berserk and pushed me backwards. I straightened up and told him again to leave. You were just walking in the door. He smacked me hard and you tore into him. I saw you get a few licks in, but then he flat beat you to a pulp. I want to thank you from the bottom of my heart. If you had not intervened, I'm afraid that man would have killed me."

"According to O'Phalon, you saved his life," repeated Martha. "He said he had never been hit so hard."

"You take whatever time you need to recover; we will make do." said O'Phalon. "And whatever you do, don't go shoot him, the sheriff warned us both. He and a lot of his deputies are going up to Greenville tomorrow to arrest him."

"Just rest." said Martha. "I will look in on you later."

They both left with the lamp still lit. What I noticed next was my rifle in its proper place across two pegs above my bed, where I left it. Below it, hanging on the single peg was my gun belt where it wasn't. Someone had taken it off me and placed it where it belonged, close to hand.

Chapter 12

—————▼—————

Pity money, that's what it was. My morning tips totaled over four dollars and change. I had one eye shut and plenty of facial bruising. The bandage covering the doctor's stitching added to the look. At least the money would help cover the doctor's fee, whatever it was.

Little would it do however, for my aches and pains which I endured as I finished up my morning duties at Martha's.

"It's coming, the wagon is coming!" yelled out a customer seated close to the window.

Everyone, Martha and I included, went out the door to see the sheriff's wagon as it passed by.

Actually, there were three conveyances, two wagons and a nice buggy. The first wagon was being driven by a deputy; the sheriff sat the seat. On a make shift board seat in the rear, sat a manacled Derek Garrison.

Behind that wagon came another with four more deputies.

Following those, was a fine black buggy, pulled by beautiful a black horse. A big, mean-looking man drove the buggy.

As they passed by, I saw two things of merit. First, I saw Derek Garrison give an obvious nod to Big Ben. Ben returned the gesture. Garrison paid no never mind to the gawkers. He did, however, make eye contact with me. As he did, he either smiled or sneered, which I did not know. What he revealed was a gap in his front teeth. At least two of which were missing. The injury was fresh as just a small dribble of blood was still rolling off his lower lip.

"The posse bloodied him," said a man.

"Don't think so," said another. "None of the deputies show sign of injury."

"Someone's in big, big trouble." said the first man.

"Who is driver the buggy?" Martha asked.

"That's Garrison's foreman."

"His foreman?" questioned another.

"Yes, that's him. Garrison has several thousand acres up in Greenville. He is as wealthy as he is vicious. He didn't get all he has by being Mr. Nice Guy. That buggy is to take him back home once he posts his bond. They won't have him in jail more than a few minutes."

As most returned to their breakfast, a monster hand squeezed my shoulder. It was Big Ben.

"Come see me tonight at the office when you finish up here at the restaurant." he said.

"Yes, sir."

He said no more and walked up the road towards the mill.

All the rest of the day as I did my labors, I wondered what Big Ben wanted to talk to me about. I had grown, but I'd no desire to work the mill, I had done the math. His mill workers made two dollars a day, but when one figured in my room and board arrangement, which I would lose, I would be losing money. As it was now, I had no real expenses except for ammunition and clothes. My ammunition costs were offset by selling game for the table and my clothing was mostly second hand.

The sun was setting as I rapped politely on the office door. Through the glass, I could see Big Ben behind his lamp lite, paper strewn desk.

"Come in, Cal." he said. "Close the door, have a seat."

I took the chair in front of the desk.

"I had you come by to tell you a story."

Relieved I was, as I had a practiced excuse for refusing employment.

"That Derek Garrison is a long remembering, vengeful sort, I know him well. You are in danger, and I'm not sure what to do about it."

"Yes, sir," I responded, unsure still where this conversation was going.

"To start, you can't fight for spit, Cal. Oh, you are game, you sure enough got a good lick in, but you don't have the mechanics nor the bulk to win. That man will clean your clock again, just like he did yesterday, only worse. Those teeth will never grow back, and he won't forget. He will not let it lie, it's not his way. It's not so much his teeth, it's more his ego."

"Yes, sir." I responded again probably with more concern in my voice.

"Those peashooters you carry will just irate him."

"Do I need a bigger gun?"

"No, no. This is more complicated than that. You shoot him, the law will get you. It would be murder. This is 1880, the world is tamer, the law will find you, maybe even hang you."

"I could go on the run, I've some money set aside."

"No, I think he would have you hunted down. The man has more money than God and he made it fighting. He was a pugilist you know."

"Pugilist?" I questioned.

"He was a professional fighter and built up both reputation and fortune which he has invested wisely. He is a man used to having life his way. All matters have a physical resolution. He is the power and all others bend to his will, all but one."

"One?"

"Yes, only one man has ever bested him in a toe-to-toe, me and he knows I could do it again. He needs a whipping, but I made a promise."

"Promise?" he had my attention.

"Yes, I promised our now dead mother I'd never fight him again."

"Our mother?"

"Yes, Derek is my half-brother by Mom's second husband. We grew up together. His dad had bulk, mine had more."

"What do you want from me?" I asked.

"I want your promise not to shoot the bastard. He is my mother's son. He will come for you, make no mistake, but it will not be right away. He will need time for memories to fade, but you can count on it, he will come."

"I guess I will have to hit the road again."

"Or you could stay, let me help you, train you, get you ready, at least to the point where he can't kill you. You have both stamina and heart. He as experience and bulk. His strength is waning, he's not as strong as he was. You my boy, are only getting stronger."

I could shoot, but he was right about fighting. I'd had two fights in my life and lost them both. If I was going west, maybe it was a skill I could use.

"What do I need to do and when do we start?"

"Tomorrow night after work, come here, then every night and Sundays until we are ready. You game?"

"I'm game."

Chapter 13

▼

There was a lamplit room in the back of the mill, maybe 12 foot by 24 foot. Within it was a wood stove blazing away, hot was the air. Hanging from the ceiling was a punching bag and a big canvas sack filled with something. Five or six pairs of padded boxing gloves hung from hooks along the wall. There was a bench with bars of all sizes and heavy-looking weights.

"This is my work-out gym." said Big Ben, "Dennis will be joining us soon. He's an employee who likes to work out. He went home for dinner."

"Yes, sir." I said.

"We start every night with stretching exercises, then basic calisthenics, some weight work, some sparing then some bag work. We will go easy at first, but as we move along, I want you to give it your best and then some. The work outs will run about two hours, Sunday we will play by ear. From now on, if you go anywhere, run. It will do you well to take a run every night after we are finished. You want strength and stamina."

Big Ben was showing me stretching exercises when Dennis came in. Dennis was older than me, maybe twenty, he was a little taller and heavier.

"You must be Cal Cole," he said as he joined us. "Ben told me about you getting bashed by Derek. Glad it wasn't me, not yet at least."

The routine we went through left me soaked with sweat. Both were patient, both used encouragement as I was shown what to do.

When we were finished for the night, Big Ben said to take a run, that we would meet tomorrow night.

As directed, I jogged a mile down the dark rock-walled road, saw a bear, and ran a whole lot faster back.

For months and months, the routine was the same, each night Big Ben giving us lesson in pugilism. How to stand, how to move, how to anticipate, block and counter. More importantly, he taught us how to punch, to punch through, and to punch hard.

Dennis was good and he wacked me plenty as we sparred early on, but I learned quick and often rocked his world. He'd wipe the swear out of his eyes, laugh, spit, and come at me again. We became good friends.

One night after the workout as we were going out the front door, he said, "Hey Cal, why don't you skip your run and come home with me. I want you to meet Sara Sue, the girl I live with."

"Ok," I said, "But I think I should go home and clean up first."

"No, don't bother, she knows how sweaty we get. It's no problem. Come on."

We jogged to his place, maybe a full mile west of town.

The house sat by itself well off the road. It was modest at best. From the outside it appeared to have a main room, with a garret room above and a lean to annex on one side. Just a house, it was no more.

Inside were two women, one he introduced as Sara Sue, the other, I already was familiar with, Amelia.

"Girls, this is my friend, Cal Cole." He said.

I don't know how Sara Sue reacted as my eyes were on Amelia. Amelia had just the faintest hint of a smile as she reached out and took my hand.

"Pleased to finally meet you Cal Cole."

"Yes, ma'am." was all I could say.

"Do we have any ale?" he asked Sara.

"Of course."

"Well, get Cal a glass, bring mine into the bath."

"Bath?" I asked.

"Yes, we have a real bathtub, the waters hot and I'm first."

Sara sue produced four glasses of ale and put two of them on the table for Amelia and I, then took the other two into the annex where Dennis had vanished.

Amelia and I sat the table. I sipped the ale, my first ever, and pretended I had drunk it before. She obviously had. We had some idle prater, could hear splashing and laughter from the other room. As we talked, I saw Amelia as I had years ago, she hadn't changed a bit.

We finished the ale. Amelia got up and got two more. We had almost finished the second when Dennis and Sara Sue came from the annex room clad in no more than towels. They were laughing as Dennis followed her up the ladder to the loft. Once up there, two towels were thrown down.

"It's all yours, Cal."

They were gone, but I could hear activity above. At this point in time, I wished I was being pounded by Derek, anything, anywhere but where I was. Nervous was an understatement.

"Well," said Amelia, as she went for the towels, "you coming to the bath or not?"

Not a word came out of my lips. I just followed her into the candle lit annex. What I had remembered, I saw again.

What I did not know, was learned; over and over. Amelia was a good teacher in all regards.

Chapter 14

▼

It was the very next day, sorting the post, I came across a letter addressed to Calvin Coleman C/o Reginal Post Master Rindge, New Hampshire. There was a note written across the front to O'Phalon from Richard Gates, the postmaster of Rindge. All it said was, "No Calvin Coleman down here, but some folks said you might have one up there." There was no return address, Postmark was Dodge City, Kansas.

In hand was my very first letter. I pulled my sheath knife and carefully cut it open. It read,

"Dear Calvin,

I pray this letter finds you hale and hearty. After the Gordan affair, we were forced to flee before I could tell you about the feelings that I had for you. I'm not sure they have ever changed. At least I thought about you after. What has changed are our names. The family has been on the move for these many years. We believe there are warrants for father, and of course the Gordan boys keep seeking our whereabouts. They are a vengeful bunch, happy to shoot my father or abuse me again. So, we move and keep moving and thus far, have eluded them both. I'm a full-grown woman now, but with the life we live, constantly on the move, I've had no time to make new friends or even meet other boys. I'm lonely and miss our home, simpler times, and the best friend I almost never had.

Jen"

I was floored. I had no idea she had ever had feelings for me. We were just kids. I wanted to immediately write her back, but I had no address, I didn't even know her name.

The only clue I had was Dodge City, Kansas. Either she or someone she knew post marked this letter from Dodge. It had taken five weeks for the letter to make its way to Peterborough. Five weeks ago, Jen might have been in Dodge City, Kansas. She could be anywhere, but probably somewhere out west.

I went back to work sorting the mail, but my thoughts were to Jenny and what problems she and her family were having. O'Phalon was about to tell me something, when the sheriff came in the door.

"Good news and bad news, men." he said, looking at me. "Cal, you are sure gaining weight and muscle. Where did that beard come from? Well, maybe it's just as well, you sure don't look like a mild-mannered school boy no more."

"What is the news, Sherriff?" asked O'Phalon. "Not much happens around here."

"The good news is that Derek Garrison plead guilty to battery for striking you in the face. He paid a seven-dollar fine and was warned to never bother you again."

"What about beating up Cal here?"

"It was a negotiated settlement. As Garrison's attorney explained to the State's attorney, Derek was indeed guilty of losing his temper and hitting you, but once he did, it was over. He was about to apologize when Cal here attacked him from behind and smashed out his teeth. He was after that, only defending himself from a crazed teenager. The state's attorney bought his logic and settled out of court. The case was closed.

I came to tell you in person and to warn you, Cal, not to go shoot Derek. I'd have to run you in. Since it's already in the record and recognized as true by the state of New Hampshire that you are a crazed teenager who already knocked Garrison's teeth out, his getting shot will certainly lead to your arrest and no mercy from the court. Do you understand?"

"Yes, sir."

The sheriff left and O'Phalon grumbled about Garrison the rest of the afternoon. He was still cussing when I left for Martha's. Mentally, I was cursing too.

After Martha's it was back to Big Ben's. Dennis met me at the door.

"Good time last night, Cal?"

"Yes, it was."

"Want to do it again?"

"Sure."

"Well, forget it. Amelia left for home this morning. She lives down near Boston now, but she'll be back up for another visit. She asked if I would invite you home again when she did."

I almost said something when Dennis continued, "Don't get a big head lover boy. She'd be happy whoever I brought home. Amelia has never been particular. You should be."

It was a typical workout to start followed by Ben's instruction as we sparred.

"Feet, feet!" he said, "move those feet, plant, punch, move, hook, hook, plant, punch!"

Ben was really pushing us. Poor Dennis was getting the bejesus pounded out of him. He was good, but I was getting so much better.

"Take a break, boys." Ben ordered. "Catch your breath.

"Both of you can box, now I'm going to teach you to fight. The object is to survive, to win. Marquess of Queensberry rules only apply behind the ropes. Here on, it's knuckles and skull, whole hog or die."

And that's the way it was. Where to damage a man. How to hit and where to kick, bite, or butt. Then it was how to and when to wrestle.

Over the next couple of months, we learned it all.

I hit the scale at 189 and it was all new muscle. Dennis went 215.

One night after practice, Big Ben said, "I think I have taught you boys all I can about fighting. You are both good, damn good. I'd hate to fight either one of you. It's time for your baccalaureate exorcise. Come back tomorrow night."

Chapter 15

▼

Late I was getting to Big Ben's baccalaureate whatever it was. There were extra to-do's at Martha's, that and a few late diners. I found Ben and Dennis seated at the lamp-lit desk.

"Come on in, Cal. Have a seat," smiled Ben. "Here, have a taste of this, I've been saving it for tonight, Kentucky Bourbon."

Ben poured a small amount into a small glass. He and Dennis already had theirs.

"Bourbon is a whisky. It is to be sipped in moderation. All liquor is to be taken in moderation. Only a fool drinks to excess. That is lesson one."

I sat back and took a sip as directed and near choked as the fire ran down my throat.

"It's a bit harsh at first," he chuckled, "but you'll appreciate it."

I wasn't so sure and allowed my insides to recover before I attempted another.

"This is your graduation, there is nothing else to teach you. I have a present for you both."   He reached under the desk and pulled out two oak ax handles. He tossed one to Dennis, one to me.

"If all else fails, use these!"

He was roaring with laughter, that contagious laugh that had Dennis and I joining him.

When finally, the laughter abated, Big Ben began, "I was married once, nice woman, but she bore me no children. Then she up and died on me. I had loved her so much no other could have taken her place. I remained as I am, a big, lonely man.

"You boys, Dennis, Cal, are the closest to sons I will ever have. I have watched each of you go about your lives before making my decision to bring you into mine. I put you through hell to mold you into the men I think you should be." He took another sip of his drink.

"I will tell you now, I had different reasons for each of you. First, I need someone to inherit my business, someone to love it as I do and keep it alive. Dennis, that's you. I've watched you work like a dog. You know everything there is to know except how to give orders rather than take them. Tomorrow you report as the foreman. One year from now, the mill is yours." Then he looked at me.

"Cal, my reasons for opening up my heart to you are twofold. First, I just flat liked you, from the day you walked in the door and asked for a job. I saw you make Martha's life more pleasurable and O'Phalon a success. You were half the size you are now and you did the work of two people, maybe more. But, kid, you couldn't fight for spit. You always said you were going west, now go prepared. You are a man to walk the mountains with." He took yet another sip from his glass as did I.

"The second reason was my selfishness for sure. I wanted you to have no idle time. I wanted to keep you busy. I wanted you so dog ass tired you would not have the strength or wear with all to sneak off and shoot that bastard brother of mine." Then he turned to Dennis.

"Dennis, ten percent of the annual profits are to be Cal's for as long as the mill exists. It's been arranged with the bank. The money will go into the account of Cal Cole to be redeemed as Cal or his heirs choose. The other ninety percent is for you and your heirs. Oh, Dennis, marry Sara and soon. She looks pregnant to me. Nice lady, I think. At least she makes you smile."

"Cal, you go see that big world out there. You got the money, can't fool me. I bet you've a thousand dollars stashed."

I had that and a lot more.

We sipped our bourbon and talked.

"Now there are a few other tidbits of wisdom I need to pass, things to never forget," Ben said.

"First, never hit a lady. Never pick or start a fight, but then again, never let yourself get hit first. Never boast, brag, or threaten. If you are going to fight, be the first with the most. Just do it."

"Remember, it is okay to walk away. It's okay to run. Discretion is the better part of valor."

"Friends are forever. You boys remember that. Come hell or high water, keep your bond. And both of you remember, dig your posts deep, drink up stream of the herd, and never shit in your own nest."

We all went to laughing again and had one more bourbon, which by now I had a liking for.

As we got up to leave, Ben reached out to shake our hands.

"Proud of you both, very proud."

As he clasped mine in that huge mitt of his, he said, "Tomorrow go up to the bank, there are a few papers for you to read and sign. There is also another legal matter there for you to address. I do not know what it is."

"Yes, sir."

That night I thought of many things. Big Ben and how indebted to him I was to him, Martha and her restaurant, O'Phalon and the Postal Freight business, Dennis and Sara, Amelia and her teachings. But mostly I thought about that first that kiss and the girl who gave it, Jen.

Usually I read before bed. I was surprised I had not read the inked words right off the pages of those western dime novels I had collected. This night I read not a single word. I cut the light and fell asleep in my most comfortable world.

Chapter 16

▼

The bank was a fortress. It was small, but built with granite boulders, and small slit type windows too small for a man to crawl through. There was only one entrance, the front door. There were two doors, the outside door swung outward. It was made with heavy timbers. The inside door was conventional, it swung in. The roof was slate. Many times, I had been in the business, as I often times made deposits for Martha and O'Phalon.

Across the front was an interior stone-wall divider with a barred service window. Beyond the divider were two desks and beyond, a heavy iron safe.

"Good morning, Cal." Greeted Alice, the village gossip queen. She knew everyone as well as their business. She was a regular at the restaurant.

"I'm here to see Mr. Whitaker."

"Vernon, Cal's here to see you."

"Let him in. Come on back, Cal."

The door opened and I entered the office section.

"Sit, Cal, sit here. We have two different items to deal with."

"Yes, sir."

"First there is paperwork to sign. Ben has requested we open a bank account for you into which periodic deposits will be made. I have everything ready."

He produced three different papers and had me sign my name. I wrote "Cal Cole" three times. He signed another and gave it to me.

"This is your bank account into which deposits can be made. I will need some coin to actually open the account. Have you some money?"

"Yes, sir, but I will have to go get it."

"Okay, you can bring your coin back later."

"If there is money in my account, how can I get to it?"

"Just walk in, we will know our account number. Ask and we will give it to you."

"What if I'm away, maybe in another town or state. How do I get my money?"

"When that happens, we do a bank-to-bank transaction. This day and age, with the telegraph system, it is really simple. A bank would wire us and verify you have adequate funds to cover the request at the other end. We could wire back and verify. That bank would give you the cash and we would send the actual money to them."

"How does the money get from here to where ever?"

"Wells Fargo."

"And if Wells Fargo gets robbed, how does the other bank get their money?"

"Wells Fargo signs for the cash and makes restitution if the money is stolen. They guarantee delivery. It's all modern and efficient."

"Do you guarantee the money in your safe?"

"Well," he hummed, "actually, no."

"If I get robbed, we all lose. But I can assure you, your coin and the money you get from the mill is as safe in this building as I can make it."

"What if I have a lot of money?"

"You mean several coins?"

"Exactly."

"Then I would suggest you invest in something, businesses, bonds, stocks, or real estate. Cash in the bank is basically worthless. The interest we pay is next to nil. If you invest wisely you could make money by allowing entities to use your money."

"Sounds complicated." I said.

"Well, that's down the road. We don't know what your Mill deposits will be, and the coin to open your account will be needed in the account to keep it open."

"How much coin will I need to open?"

"I'll do it for a dollar or two."

'Okay, I'll be right back."

"We can finish the other matter first."

"No, sir. This one comes first. I'll be right back."

I left, went to my room and pulled four flour sacks of coin from under my bed. I wasn't exactly sure what I had, but it was well over a dollar a day for these past four years. I was guessing $1,400 to $1,500.

The coin was heavy. I grabbed a two wheeled cart from the freight house, loaded my coin and pushed it over to the bank.

"What's that, Cal?" he asked as I walked back into the office.

"My coin."

"All of it?"

"Yes, sir. Near $1,500 I'm sure."

That banker man near fell over. He was speechless as he looked through the four sacks.

"My God, boy! Where did this come from?"

"I worked for it."

"You saved this much cash?"

"Yes, and like you said, I need my coin to open an account. Here it is."

"Alice, Alice! Count these bags of coin"

"Today?"

"Yes, start counting and don't go home until it's done."

Alice was no longer smiling. My guess she would be pulling an all-nighter.

Mr. Whitaker was still gawking at the flour sacks.

"You made that much swamping a restaurant?"

"Well, yes. But some came from the Post and Freight business, the rest from shooting squirrels."

"Squirrels you say?"

"Don't we have other business?"

"Oh, yes," he said, still looking at the flour sacks. "Squirrels you say. There can't be a damn squirrel alive east of the Mississippi."

We returned to the desk. I could see Alice was not happy.

"We have a letter here from a lawyer's office in Payson, Arizona Territory. Do you know Mr. Robert R. Russell?"

"No, sir."

"Well, he knows you."

"He does?"

"Well, he did. You are apparently the beneficiary of his estate; more than fifty thousand acres, house, horse barn and livestock."

"What?"

"This is huge, lad!"

He was reading as he talked, "Mr. Robert R. Russell, blah blah blah, bequeaths it all to Calvin Coleman, son of Nadine and Horace Coleman, Fitzwilliam, New Hampshire. That's you, isn't it?"

"Yes."

"The actual will and deed are in the safe of David Alan Beam, Attorney of Law, Payson, Arizona.

"Payson?"

"I never heard of it either, but there is a catch. You have a calendar year upon this service, which I'm to verify, to respond in person in Payson."

"Looks like a road trip." I responded.

"There is another catch."

"What's that?"

"You have to produce for inspection a Remington-Rider rifle and a Smith and Wesson pistol that Robert Russell gave you as a gift. Beam has the serial numbers. They must be the same weapons and numbers and will be used to verify the presenter is, in fact, Calvin Coleman."

Uncle Bob. I told myself. Uncle Bob had died. Uncle Bob had left me his estate.

That night after work, as I left Martha's, the lamp was still lit in the bank. The next morning on my way back to Martha's, I saw Mr. Whitaker and Alice locking up the bank.

Whitaker saw me and waved me over. I joined him in the front of the bank.

"All night we counted then counted again. You did not have $1,500. You had $1,734.01."

"Mr. Whitaker, I will come get some for traveling money. I trust you to keep the rest for me."

"I will, rest assured. But travel carefully. If anyone else knows about those guns, you'll have trouble."

"Does Alice know?"

"No, she's a blabber mouth, but she can count coins, over and over. She's not happy.

"We are done, closed for the day." He said as he flipped the closed sign over on the door. "I'm going to bed."

Chapter 17

▼

At breakfast, I told Martha that this was my last week. I thanked her over and over for the last four years of employment. All she did was cry.

"If you can hire a replacement for me, I can spend the time training them."

"I knew when you came here you would someday be leaving," She said. "I just didn't know I would come to love and rely on you."

I left with a guilt trip to work for O'Phalon's. When I gave him a week's notice, he shrugged his shoulders and just went silent. He didn't cry but his voice quivered when he finally spoke.

"Cal," he said, "I understand completely. You told us four years ago you were on the road, off to see the world. There is more to life than sorting the mail and sweeping the floor in Peterborough, New Hampshire. Even if I set you up as Postmaster here, it's a mundane life at best. It's a big world out there. Go see it with my love and respect. You were the son I never had. Just remember you can always come back."

Then I went to see Big Ben. Dennis was in the office with him. I told them about Arizona and an inheritance that I intended to claim.

"I knew you were leaving someday, but it's hard to watch you actually go. You have come to mean so much to us."

"Yes, you have, Cal. The brother I almost never had." said Dennis.

Ben then asked, "How will you travel?"

"I'm not sure. There are stage coaches and trains."

"You know, Ben said, "If I were young and I wanted to see the world, I'd get me a horse and just mosey my way west. You'll see more, meet more people and maybe find your heart's desire between here and Arizona."

"You might stop by Boston," winked Dennis.

Then he started laughing as did I.

I asked Ben where I could purchase a traveling horse and gear. He directed me to a stable up by Lake Nubanusit. Said to use his name.

I went back to the bank and talked with Vernon Whitaker again. On my previous visit he had whispered to me the requirement of presenting my 22 caliber weapons to receive my inheritance. I thought I might trust him.

We discussed investments and things he might be able to do with my money. I took seven hundred dollars for traveling funds and left the rest for him to invest for a percentage. I had some concern, but nothing ventured, nothing gained. He was also directed to invest any money received from the mill profits.

Whitaker assured me that if I ever needed cash, I was to send him a wire, but we needed some kind of pass word to verify that it was me making the request. Something simple that only he and I would know.

I thought for a second and said, "22 Cal Cole."

Sunday as I jogged up to Lake Nubanusit, as directed by Ben, I passed literally hundreds of horses and many a sign saying, "Horses for Sale." I stopped at none and held to my destination.

The sign said, "Pleasant Valley Stables, Luther Rosecram, Proprietor."

Once past the barking dogs, I knocked the door to the house. It opened and a man stuck his head out, looked at me, searched the area, then looked at me again.

"Yes?" he questioned.

"My name, sir, is Cal Cole and I would like to purchase a horse and tack."

"You have money?"

"Of course."

"Well, follow me." He was smiling.

I was led to a larger than normal stable at the rear. Behind the stable were three dry lots with as many as twenty horses mulling about within. There were six or seven horses per lot.

We stopped on lot one.

"These here are my low-end budget horses. They are all sound, but have some age on them. What are your pans for the animal?"

Travel, sir."

"How far?"

"The west."

We moved to the next pen.

He was smiling again. "Now, this group is younger, but well broke, mind you. That bay, now she's a walker, she'll go all day on a handful of grass.

"What is your experience with horses?"

"About none, sir. Our family only had one, an old buggy horse. I fed her for around three years."

"You said you had money."

"Yes, I do."

We moved to the third pen.

"Now these are real travelers, broke to ride and not yet barn sour. The Black with three white stockings would be my first choice."

As I looked them over, they all looked alike, pen one, two, and three. They were horses was all I could say.

"No experience, money, and a desire to be a long way from here. Quick, I'd expect. Family here?"

"Yes, and no. They have died off or moved away."

He was almost giddy.

"Now if I were you, I would pick that white blazed sorrel, he's a beaut'."

"He is a good-looking horse." I responded, but I had seen right off he was a mare.

It was at that point I knew I was being bilked and was out of my league. I had heard once about the wily horse trader. I had one here. I wondered why Ben had sent me here.

"I don't know sir; one horse is the same as another to me. I was referred here by my friend who said you would treat me fair and give me the best you had."

"And who is your friend. Maybe I know him?"

"Big Ben, the mill owner in Peterborough."

The trader's smile went immediately to an out and out sneer.

"Big Ben, the rotten, no-good son of a bitch?"

"Yes, sir, I guess."

"He said I would treat you fair and square and give you the best?"

"He did."

"That rotten bastard, no-good son of a bitch?"

"I guess, but he seemed to hold your horse opinion in high regard."

"I bet he did."

The man was mad, instantly mad, totally enraged. I thought he might even strike out at me, though a mistake for sure he'd be making.

"Follow me." he said.

We went into the actual stable. There were at least ten stalls each with a horse in it. We skipped nine of them and went to the tenth.

He went in and came out leading a magnificent gelding. He was tall, well built, and coal oil black. He tied it to the stall gate, walked to his tack room and returned with a saddle, blanket and bridle, all of which he affixed to the animal.

As he labored, I could hear constant muttering, all profanity.

Once finished, he said, "Now here he is, the best of the best. Did Ben tell you how much to pay?"

"No, sir. He said you were a fair man."

"That no-good bastard. Eighty-five dollars, that's my best price for my best horse with tack, not a penny less."

"I will tell him."

"Make it seventy-five dollars, tell him that."

"I will."

I paid Rosecram the seventy-five dollars, then with the deal made and the reins in hand, I lead my horse from the stable.

"You be sure to show Ben the horse." He said, "and tell him the price. I sold him a horse once that went lame before he got it home. That rotten bastard brought it back and showed me what God loves. I was six months abed."

"Yes, sir. I will."

Once seated in the saddle and moving south along the road, I knew I had the best of the best. That horse could cover ground and had a liking for it.

Chapter 18

▼

I finished out by time at Martha's and O'Phalon's as given. Both had found a replacement. Martha had procured a chubby fourteen-year-old girl with a perpetual smile. O'Phalon hired an old man with no teeth. My last two days were teaching both the tricks of the trade, few there were.

Then for two days I made purchases and packed for my trip west. Hardest to find was a saddle scabbard for my rifle but I found one. My greatest purchase was a real sleeping bag, it was a revelation to me. One simple rolled it out and you snuggled down in it. Downy filled with eider feathers, the advertisement said. Two small oil cloth traps came with it, one to cover the ground, one to cover the sleeping bag.

The rest of my purchases were necessities: 22 caliber rounds, a cook kit, coffee, some jerky, a spoon, and a map.

The map was most important as I would be able to judge distances between towns where meals and lodging would be available. Looking at it, I noted that it was a long, long way to Arizona; I had less than a year to get there.

Morning came none too soon for me. I was ready to travel. I got my horse, "Black" I called him from the stables. Once tied to the freight house rail, I got him saddled and began tying my gear behind the saddle.

The locals, Martha, and O'Phalon, and gathered to see me off. There was a crowd through which emerged Derek Garrison. That foreman of his, the big, mean-looking man, sat the black buggy holding the reins of the black horse.

"I heard you were leaving and I wanted to see you off."

He was smiling and I could see his tongue between the missing teeth. He stuck out his hand as if to shake mine.

Wary I was, but I took his hand, and as I did, he clamped down hard and tried to jerk me forward as he came around with a clenched hook. I ducked as the hay maker swooshed over my head. Low like I was, I hooked back with my left and pounded his rib cage. I'd hit him good, but it was like hitting a rock wall.

He let go of my hand, let out a "Why you!" and came at me clenched and swinging. Hit me he did, but for every time he got a lick in, I got two. We sparred right there in the dirt in the middle of Peterborough.

I boxed him using every move I had learned. He came back at me using moves I hadn't.

He once more set me up for that left hook from hell. I saw the right feint, ducked and again heard the swoosh over my head as I pounded again his rib cage in the same spot. This time I hurt him; I'd broken his ribs.

He kept coming at me. I advanced and moved trying to avoid getting clenched or clobbered. He'd hit me, but the blows began to not hurt as much. His breath was becoming labored. Every chance I got I pounded his rib which he was now protecting with his right arm. He was fighting me only with his left arm.

I was breathing hard, he was gasping.

I picked a new target and worked toward that end.

I was bloody and bruised as was he, but there was no give in either. He just kept coming.

Derek momentarily dropped his right. I almost stepped in and that lowered right came up again, an upper cut that caught only my forehead. As that arm was retracting, I did move in set and drove a hard right that hit my new target, his lower front teeth.

As he recovered, I saw his teeth no more, only blood.

He came at me like a bull trying to just tackle me to the ground. I dodged and swept a leg as he went by.

Derek went to the ground. He was totally winded, no breath could he get, yet he still tried to get up.

I stepped back and drew my leg. My intention was to kick him in the head, but I was grabbed from behind by two massive arms that held me fast.

"That's enough, Cal." said a familiar voice. "That's enough, it's over."

Big Ben had me lifted off the ground. He spun me around and set me down.

"It's over." he said again.

Glad I was too. My whole body hurt. I was covered in blood, mostly mine. My gasping for air did little to fill my lungs.

The crowd that had been twenty was now fifty. They had watched as one man tried to beat another to death and the other trying not to die.

Big Ben and the foreman sat Derek in the buggy seat. As the foreman turned the rig, we made eye contact. It wasn't over, and fists would not be the weapon of choice, of that I was sure.

Chapter 19

Two days I laid abed. The man had hurt me plenty. I had taken a pounding. Big Ben had been right, I had youth, stamina, and some skill, but I had fought a man and I knew it.

Early on the third day I left just before dawn, no fanfare this time. When the town woke up, I would be gone.

The sun was just breaking over my left shoulder as I made the turn in Jaffrey. My intention was to stop and see Mell, her place not five miles further.

A mile out of Jaffrey, I could see a buggy backed into the trees. A man appeared to be sleeping on the seat. A drunkard no doubt, who did not make it home. I paid him no heed as I was liking my animal and the pace. At the speed the horse effortlessly maintained I could be in Kansas by morning.

Not twenty yards from the carriage, the man looked up and flipped the whip to that horse, drove it into the road, thereby blocking easy passage. He was out of the buggy in but a thrice pointing a long gun at me. Our distance was but a few yards. It was Derek's foreman and he was leveling his weapon at me.

Instinctively that twenty-two caliber Smith was in my hand and I was firing rounds. I'm not sure if he was hit by the first as he got a shot off, which hit first the pommel on my saddle before it hit me low, but I was positive my next six hit the man where he lived.

The foreman dropped his rifle and held his chest with both hands. He fell to his knees, then to his face.

He was alive, but hurt bad.

I dismounted, tied off my horse, and approached. He wasn't dead and was trying to get up. I booted him over on his back. I'd sure enough put holes in him, all center chest. There was plenty of bleeding too.

"You shot me, you son of a bitch! You shot me!"

"Yup. You just hang on now. Soon as I reload, I'm going to shoot you seven more times."

"No, no, don't shoot no more! I think you already killed me."

"Seven more ought to do it, I think."

"No, no more!"

That was it for the foreman as he said no more. He was either faking it or dead. The way his eyes failed to move; I was pretty sure he was dead. In his belt was a pistol. I took it out. It was a Smith and Wesson, just like mine, only it was a thirty-eight caliber.

I stuck it in my belt, mounted up and road. Leaving the foreman as he lay, his rifle still next to him. No one had seen me as far as I knew. There was a logging trail which cut through the mosquitos and came out near Mell's place. I took it, reloading my pistol as I rode.

The injury to my belly was not a bullet, but a piece of the pommel that had wacked me hard. I wasn't bleeding but I would have an additional bruise to add to those I still carried.

Mell was bent over hoeing in her garden when I rode up. She was so involved in her labors she never even looked up until the horse snorted.

"Well look who is here." she said as she turned. "If it isn't Cal Cole, all grown up. And all beat up as usual.

"Get off that monster and give me a hug. You're a sight for sore eyes you are"

"And you too, Mell." I said getting down.

She was in both regards. She was beautiful and my eyes still hurt from the fight.

"You on the run again?" she asked jokingly.

"Well, matter of fact, I am. I'm not sure what I'm running from, less sure where I'm running to."

"Headed for the hide out?"

"No, I'm going a bit farther. I'm off to the see the world, or at least as far as the Arizona Territory."

"Did you eat?"

"Not yet."

"I've got coffee and apple pie."

"Yes, ma'am." and I meant it.

Mell and I sat the steps as I ate, drank and talked. I told her about getting an inheritance from Uncle Bob in Arizona and my pending trip to claim it. I mentioned getting a letter from Jen and some of the details, especially having no name or address.

"She's in peril and there is no way to help."

"You can't help everyone, Cal, and from the looks of you, if you don't stop fighting there will be no help for you either."

"Seems so." I really enjoyed talking to her but after an hour I took my leave.

I got my hug and kiss goodbye, climbed up on the Black and hit the trail south by southwest. I'd miss all my friends in Peterborough, but I'd miss Mell the most. As I rode, I even mused, if Mell was younger, or if I were older, or if she wasn't married, or if I wasn't off to claim my inheritance, or if I wasn't secretly trying to find Jen, I probably wouldn't bother going anywhere. Just so many "or if's" in life.

Nightfall came in Massachusetts and I'd seen no posse. So far so good.

Twelve night-falls later I was watching the sunset across Lake Erie. It looked like an ocean to me, vast and blue. Those past thirteen days I had rode through some beautiful country. There were mountains, valleys, streams, and rivers, but there were towns and farms almost continuously. Nice people, too. All welcoming, especially if you had some coin to spend.

That horse I rode loved to travel. Rosecram could sure pick them. I worked the horse around ten hours a day. I'd ride all morning, graze at noon, then ride another five hours before seeking a place to stay. Only one night did I camp. I calculated we averaged around fifty miles per day.

Two days later, I found an inn with rooms just south of Cleveland. I took a room, stashed my gear, and stalled the Black with both hay and grains.

What I wanted was a meal. As I was the only customer that night, the owner gave me all of his attention. Nice fellow he was, just a peach.

He served steak and potatoes, much to my pleasure.

After the meal, he asked if I wanted a drink. Not knowing what else to order, I just said, "Bourbon."

"A fine choice, just a fine choice. Mind if I join you?"

"Not at all."

He brought two glasses to the table each with a chunk of ice. In the other hand, he had a bottle of what said, "Kentucky Bourbon."

"Finally," he said, "a man comes in and asks for a civilized drink."

He filled both glasses.

"Here," he said, raising his glass, "a toast to your health and the man who distilled this wonderful drink."

"Here, here!" I responded and we touched our glasses.

The first sip was far from harsh, it was as the man said, civilized. Our conversation was pleasant, just this and that's.

"What's your name?" he asked.

"Cal Cole."

"The Cal Cole from up New Hampshire way?"

"Yes."

"The same Cal Cole that bested Derek Garrison in a toe to toe about two weeks ago?"

"I guess."

"Well, let me buy you another drink. It came over the telegraph wire not a week ago that some young kid named Cal Cole beat the famous heavy weight title holder in a dirty street fight. Is it true?"

"I guess so, I'm here and he's not."

"Damn.

"Tell me about it."

"Nothing to tell. We fought, he lost."

Lucky for me, the man changed the subject back to this and that's.

"You know, you aren't the first from lower New Hampshire to come through here. Three young ruffians came through two years ago. Mean lads they were. We had just the nicest family working here. The girl caught glimpse of them and she was gone. The next day we couldn't find hide nor hair of that family.

"Know their names?" I asked.

"The Andersons; Richard, Mary, and Elizabeth. Richard worked at the lumber yard, Mary and Elizabeth filled here at the inn."

"Let me ask you," I questioned. "Three things I need to know. Was Richard missing fingers on one hand? Was Mary beautiful beyond all words and did Elizabeth compare with her mother?"

"Why, yes to all three."

"Did the men have names."

"Well, we think they did, but the sheriff never learned their last name."

"Sheriff?"

"Oh yeah, after the lumber yard owner was found murdered the whole town started putting our heads together. We remembered that those men called themselves by name: John, Ralph, and Richie. They were sure interested in the whereabouts of the Andersons. They were here, Ole Man McTavish was murdered and they were all gone."

"Did you see the men?" I asked.

"No, I didn't, but my wife did. She said they were big boys, maybe in their late teens or early twenties. They all had scraggly beards and wore pistols. She only saw them in passing but she remembered one was shorter, fat and walked with a limp."

"Their last name was Gordan." I said. "Do you know which way they went?"

"They were last seen on the road to Dayton."

Chapter 20

South by southwest I rode. The landscape was changing. The hills were not as big, the trees were no longer pine. Broadleaf trees had replaced them. The farms were bigger, almost continuous. I had not seen a stone fence for hundreds of miles. Post and wire had replaced them. I had not even seen a stone. The roads were either dirt or mud. The small towns with diners and inns were more plentiful. The people were still amicable, always glad to provide a service for a coin or seven. A traveler got what he paid for.

Much thought was given to the Prescott, now Anderson, family. The revelation that the Cleveland inn had to be a chance encounter, but I learned much. First, I was several years behind them and the Gordans were still on their trail. I learned the Gordans were ruthless and had killed a man for information. I learned the family had remained together and all three were yet alive. Cleveland was a big city. Easy it would be to hide surrounded by thousands. There would be employment and resources not available in the small towns and villages.

Communication with others was easier in the cities as there were post offices and telegraphs.

Jen had written me, I wondered who else. I wondered if her father and mother did the same.

The Prescott-Andersons would need cash unless they just made it as they traveled.

By what means did they travel? Were they using coaches or trains? Maybe they had a horse or wagon. Women had baggage. They did not wear the same attire week after week.

How did the Gordans find them in Cleveland and had they found them before? Were they part blood hound, just lucky or were they being kept on the trail by someone else?

So many questions and such a vast country.

They were certainly no longer Andersons.

The one fact was the Dodge City, Kansas postmark. Dodge was on the way to Arizona.

Dayton was not much of a city, it was just a big farming town, but they had a local police department. Curiosity had me tie the horse to the rail and I went in to make some inquiries. The man at the desk wore a big star on his shirt. He was older, tall and skinny.

"Can I help you?" he asked.

"Yes, maybe." I replied. "I'm looking for some friends of mine that may have passed this way two years ago."

"Two years ago? I'm sorry, but a thousand people come through here each month. There is no way I could remember anyone that long ago."

"Well, my friends are on the run, being chased by three really bad men from up in New Hampshire. These men seem to leave dead people in their wake."

"Murderers, you say?'

"Yes, sir. The last one was in Cleveland."

"New Hampshire, Cleveland, and murder. You are ringing my bells now. And who are you and your need to know?"

"Those fleeing are my friends and I feel they are still alive, but in grave peril."

"Once again, who are you?"

"Cole, sir. Cal Cole."

"Ah, yes. We expected you. The sheriff from Lorrain Co sent us a telegraph and said to watch for you."

"They want me."

"No, not at all. He just wanted to see the last name in print. He was told that the three men wanted for murder two years ago in his county was either Jordan or Gordan."

"Gordan," I said. "John Gordan, his brother Ralph Gordan, and their cousin, Richie Gordan. Richie was the short, fat one with the limp."

"Well, thank you. I will wire this back to Lorrain Co."

"What I wanted to know, was if during that time period there were any murders or anything else related to my friends or the Gordans."

"Who are your friends?"

"Don't know. They keep changing their names."

"We did have an unrelated murder two years ago. It was a woman."

My heart sank.

"I recall she was a local, a bar maid who was found naked and dead on the road to Indianapolis. We had no suspects."

"You do now." Was all I said, walking out the door.

A week later, I was looking at a sign that said "Indianapolis." The city was immense, just huge. I asked around and was given direction to their police department. What I did not find were friendly officers willing to talk to a stranger about things that did not affect them. All I met came and went with purpose.

A few took notice of the rifle scabbard affixed to my saddle, but made no comment or asked any questions that might add to their tasks at hand.

I found a hotel, complete with a restaurant, bar, and stable. I stabled my horse, secured my gear in my room, and found a seat for dinner. Many were local diners as they came from the exterior door as opposed to the interior stair well.

The food was excellent.

After my repast, I adjourned to the bar, stood the rail and ordered a bourbon over ice. Several men, both left and right had a foot on the rail and were drinking and talking. Easy it was to become involved. I found I could manipulate the direction of conversation. We got into local crime, then into horrific crimes, then into local unsolved, horrific crimes.

"You know," said the man to my left. "we had two women killed in a three-day span about a year and a half ago. Both were whores working the south end bars. No arrests were ever made. They had suspects, but no names."

"Do you remember the dates?" I asked him.

"No, just that it was starting to get cold outside."

"I know," said the man to my right. "It was November 18th. I know it for sure as it was my daughter's birthday."

"I wish I had a daughter," I said, changing the direction of the conversation.

"Lucky me," said the man to the left, "I got four of them and no chance for fortune. Those young ladies keep my wallet empty."

"Mine do the same," said the other. "but not near so much as the wife."

Away we were talking of kids and wives.

As they compared their misfortunes, a thought came to me.

"Does Indianapolis have a library?"

"Why sure, a big one, too."

"Is it far?"

"No, not at all. Just go out the door, turn right, go six blocks. It's on the left."

"Are they open?"

"We have gas lights now, of course they're open. I think until eight or nine."

"Gentlemen, excuse me please. I've some reading I'd like to do before I retire for the night."

The library was a three-story corner building with lamp-lit windows abound. At least on the two sides I could see.

"Ma'am." I asked the lady at the desk, "have you a periodical section?"

"Why yes, we do, it's up on the third floor.

"How far back in time do your local papers go?"

"We keep them for ten years, after that only by special event."

"Thank you. How do I get up there?"

"The stairwell is over there." she said, pointing to her left, but not taking her eyes off me. The librarian was not remarkable in any regard, just a nice lady. A little older than me; she wore her hair in a bun. She had a nice smile.

When I got to the stairwell, I looked back. She was still watching me, still smiling.

"It took a bit to get the lay of it all. I looked and found the "Indianapolis Journal" issue for November 15, 1880, skipped it and pulled November 19th through 24th. I sat the desk with the five papers. Nothing is reported in real time.

The November 20th issue contained the first mention of a murder on the south side. A woman had been found in an alley, was naked and dead. No suspects were listed. November 21st the story continued. The lady was named, Betty Ward was an occasional waitress at several bars. She was last seen talking to several men unknown to staff and patrons.

November 22nd the story continued going into her dubious past, listed the cause of death as strangulation, and said three man had been interviewed but released for lack of evidence. The men were named Bill Smith, Jason Smith, and Joe Smith. All were teamsters from New Hampshire.

The November 23rd issue had "Another Southside Murder," as the headline. A woman, known prostitute, Helen Butler, was found dead in her place of business. She had been strangled. Police were looking for information.

I noticed another story in that paper, a bank robbery had occurred. I read the article. Three men wearing grain sacks over their heads did a daring daylight robbery of a bank, two employees were shot, one gravely injured. The men fled, escaping capture or identification.

"We are closing," Came a voice. "I almost forgot you were up there." said the librarian. "I just came up for the light."

"Sorry," I replied. "just let me put these papers away."

"I'll help." she said, glancing down at the articles before me. "You have an interest in murder?" she questioned.

Alarmed she was, but she showed no fear.

"Yes, ma'am. I am looking for these three murderers and a family they are following."

"You know who they are?"

"Yes, and I'm fairly confident they did a bank robbery here too."

"Oh, my. Are you a detective?"

"Sort of. I have been following two groups for several months now. I hope to find my friends before they are found by the murderers."

"Oh my," she said again, putting the papers back into their proper stack. "It seems so complicated."

"It is a long story." I replied, almost enjoying a sounding board.

"I have time," she said, "and I'd love to hear it. Murder mysteries are my passion and you are the closest to a real-life detective I've ever met. My name is Aggie."

"Cal Cole," I responded. "Would you like a cup of coffee?"

"Yes, I would. Just let me get the lights, my things, and lock up."

Aggie, it seemed to me, wanted much more than a cup of coffee and a long story. Lucky for me, she got all three.

Chapter 21

I had learned a lot. First, I was gaining on the Gordans. They were no more than two months ahead of me, maybe less. They were following a westerly track across country, leaving dead bodies wherever they stopped.

Police could be a source of information as well as bars and newspapers.

From my outlaw days up in my hide out, I remembered how lonely the life is, especially if you had money and no place to spend it. The Gordans had robbed a bank, they had cash and needed a big city within which to spend it. Big cities are the easiest place to hide. No one stands out in a crowd of strangers. In small towns, people notice everything.

The next logical city was St. Louis.

Aggie was a pleasure, no doubt about it, but she also gave me a most important clue to keep in mind. She had told me I talked funny, that I had a brogue in my speech.

"There are 'r's in words" she had laughed.

"In the Midwest and further, people pronounce the 'r,' you don't and I suspect the Gordans don't either."

"How so."

"We say, it's dark outside. You say dak. You are following men that people will notice in a conversation."

What I sought were three big men, killers who talked funny. Seemed pretty simple.

I was worried that the Gordans would find the Prescott-Andersons before

I did. It appeared to me that the family had tried many times to settle in, only to be forced to flee.

The Gordans would search every big city taking their time. When the money or the Prescott-Andersons were gone, so were they. Robbing banks or people provided the financial means for travel to the next city. The bodies left behind had been their entertainment.

It was at that point, reality took hold. Just what would I do if I actually found them? What was I going to do, call for the law? What proof of anything did I possess? Nothing. It was obvious to me I followed the trail of murderers, rapists, and robbers. Armed men they were, killers for profit, pleasure, and revenge. Who would believe me without evidence?

Me, I was armed with kid guns, a 22 single-shot rifle, a 22 pistol and a borrowed 38 pistol. I needed more firepower, a lot more. I need a rifle that would reach out and touch without putting me in jeopardy. Three pistols firing at a man with one pistol were not good odds. At least eighteen rounds would be coming at me in exchange for six going the other way. Yes, I needed a real rifle, that and a plan.

Try as I did, no plan came to mind, but in St. Louis a Winchester Model 1873 Rifle came to hand, that and 200 rounds. At the same gun shop, I traded my borrowed 38 caliber Smith and some cash for a newer model, the Frontier. It loaded 44-40 center fire cartridges, the same as the rifle. I also bought a new holster for it.

The gun shop had a shooting range out back. The owner gave me instruction as to the loading of each weapon. I found no difference in aiming and firing other than the noise and buck. The owner just looked at my targets and asked me if I wanted a job at the shop. I needed no employment as I still had over three-hundred dollars left and a mission.

Four full days I roamed about St. Louis engaging people in conversations as I attempted to learn something new. I talked with police, bartenders, patrons and especially, librarians. No luck did I have with any.

I read the newspapers and there were indeed murders. St. Louis was the rough and tumble gateway to the west and much was not unusual. There was one woman found naked in weeds down by the docks, no witnesses, suspects or obvious cause of death. Another story talked about two men had been beaten and robbed outside a river road tavern. Pistol whipped it said, and near two-hundred dollars was taken.

On the last day, I walked along checking the nicer hotels, men with money would prefer better accommodations.

At each, I used the same ruse. "Sir, I'm looking for my cousin, a short, fat fellow, my age, walks with a limp and talks funny."

I went to seven hotels. Five of the seven the clerks said, "Like you."

At the last hotel, the clerk said, "Talked just like you, an easterner for sure. There was three of them here. They raised hell, drank and whored. Paid for the first two nights up front, ran out of the third and beat us out of rent."

"What name did they give?"

"Johnsons all three. Don't remember the first names as the registry book disappeared with them, ten days ago I think."

"yup, that's my no-good cousins on my mother's side."

"You paying their bill?"

"No, sir, they owe me and I want what's mine back."

"If you get yours, bring back ours."

"I will."

It was in my mind that the Gordans were responsible, but I had no proof. The trail was down to ten days or less and they were still going west.

The next morning, I bought some new clothes, then pitched my rags. I also got a coat and a western brimmed hat. Dapper I was, at least for a few days.

Kansas City was next. It was four or five days west. My horse was well rested, strong, and as ready as he was on the first day of this two-month journey. I wondered if Rosecram had any others like him. If it wasn't so far back, I'd buy all he had.

Toward the end of my first day's travel west from St. Louis, I decided to camp somewhere. The weather was mild and I was just tired of people. That and I was growing more wary of the Gordans. I was within eight or nine days if they were real travelers., which they weren't. Their pattern was to stop for a while, rest up, spend some money, rob someone, and move on.

I had seen my first Indians that day. A sad, filthy lot they were. Two men, one woman and two small kids. They wore just rags. They had nothing else. Upon seeing me they scurried off into the brush.

They were certainly not the savage warriors of the plains I had read about, but those who had nothing would want something and had nothing to lose in an attempt to get it.

I rode on another hour. I found a small creek and rode up stream a few hundred yards. There, I found a decent camp site for the night. A squirrel barked in a tree, my 22-rifle barked back and I soon had it broiling over my small fire. I ate, crawled into that sleeping bag, and slept.

The next morning down at the stream, I was bent over about to fill my pot with water for my coffee, thinking of course about the Gordans and perils ahead, I noticed just the strangest creature floating on the surface of the water. It was a bird with a frog for a head or a frog with a bird stuck in his mouth. Both were dead.

Two things came to mind. First, Cal, don't bite of more than you can chew and second, I heard Big Ben saying, "Drink upstream from the herd." I moved and filled my coffee pot elsewhere.

Columbia, Missouri, wasn't much of a city. No police and no library, but they did have a boarding house with a room and a meal. I took both. A half a dozen people sat a long table, the meal, beef stew and biscuits. The dinner conversation was continuous throughout. The other five all seemed to know each other. Apparently, nothing ever happened in Columbia, just nothing.

I listened, nodded and when asked, responded, "New Hampshire, ma'am."

"Thought so," she said. "You talk funny."

"I knew you were from out east." Said the man across from me. "We heard you talking to Mrs. Evans earlier. Yup, never been up north, but I heard it was pretty country."

"Yes, sir it is, lots of trees, streams, lakes and mountains. Some nice people too."

"Sounds like paradise to me. "said the lady.

"I guess it is." I said surprising myself. I had never thought of it as anything but home.

After breakfast the following morning, I grabbed a few provisions from an Emporium before hitting the trail for Kansas City. According to the clerk at the store, Kansas City would be the last place to actually buy something before I went out onto what she called "that God forsaken prairie. Nothing out there but soddies and dumbass Germans. Been here years they have and still can't speak a lick of American. Stupid I tells ya, just stupid people.

She looked at me again. "You all knows you talks funny."

"I hear you, but where I come from, everyone out here sounds funny too."

We had a good laugh, then I said, "'uess I'll hit the 'ode fo' Kansas."

Chapter 22

▼

Kansas City was a miniature St. Louis, a bustling river town, with steam boats a plenty and a railway. There were houses and buildings or both sides of the river, people and activity everywhere.

On the Kansas side, I found a nicer hotel with a stable to the rear. I took a room then stabled the Black.

My evening meal I took alone at a small table in the dining room, then went to the bar for what they called a night cap. I just called it bourbon.

Crowded was the bar, eight or nine men took up all the rail space. I ordered m drink at the end and carried it to a vacant table. Only one man at the bar paid heed to my presence, an old rough looking fellow dressed in frontier garb. He wasn't tall, but he had some bulk to him. As one sized up other men, something I was prone to do, he was the only person in the room of concern.

After looking my direction three or four times, he picked up his drink and walked to my table.

"Hal Houston's my name." he said, "I've talked with these fellows and found we've not much in common. Mind if I join you?"

"By all means." I said.

"Barkeep," he bellowed, "Bring us two more over here."

He sat down and just went to talking.

"Yes, sir. I just came back east to get a taste of civilization. I do it every three or four years just to see what I'm not missing. That and buy a few things not available out on the prairie. Where are you headed?

"Out on the prairie."

"Been there before?"

"No, sir."

"Business or pleasure?"

"Business." I answered.

"That would be the only reason for sure. There is not a god damn thing pleasurable out there. Everything and everybody from here to the Pacific will either bite you, shoot you, prick you, or stick you."

"Then why do you go out there?" I asked.

"It's my home and I know nothing else."

Hal Houston talked and talked. I bought another round and then he another. We talked several hours about the trails and perils of the prairie, how to travel, when, what to watch for, and how to respond. He was a wealth of information, and he knew people. At least he claimed to. He had met all my heroes, Earp, Masterson, Holiday and Hickok. He had worked for the Cody family in Nebraska. They had a spread close to the Biehl's. The Biehl's spoke damn little English, just German mostly. They weren't much fun.

I asked him if he knew of had ever met my uncle, Bob Russell.

"Arizona Bob." He replied.

"I only knew him as Uncle Bob."

"Hell ya, I knew him. We spent a few weeks traveling together. He was headed to Arizona, said he was going to seek his fortune up under the Mogollan."

"That's him." I said.

"Good man, you resemble him. He could shoot, maybe the best shot I ever saw. All the time we traveled, we had meat on the spit and Injuns stayed way back after he dropped one off his pony at near half mile away. I wonder how he is?"

"I got a letter informing me of his death. I'm going west to see his Arizona dream; curiosity is all. Just curious."

"Dead, you say?"

"It's what the letter said."

"Well, like I said, He was a good man and as to your curiosity, I've been doing the same thing for years. I always wondered what was over there."

On and on he went until I had to excuse myself. The day had been long and I was too tired to listen.

"I like you, kid, so I got a few suggestions before you hit the grass. First, trade that new hat of yours for a worn, greasy one. Stuff those boots good and get yourself a serape like the one I wear. The more seasoned you look, the less likely you will draw attention. Besides, the slit in the serape will bring that pistol of yours quicker to hand."

"How long are you in town for?"

"Maybe a week." he said.

"Tomorrow night then," I said. "Maybe another drink or two.?

"I'd like that," he replied.

There was a bank on the same block as the hotel. The next morning, I was there when it opened. I had cash left, but Houston had told me there were few banks west of Kansas City capable of wiring money. He told me the farther I went, fewer too were accommodations or eateries. Most meals would be over a campfire or someone's soddy. Most people would be glad to share both for a coin. Money was scares on the grass. He also advised two horses or at least a ridable mule as a second mount. Many would be the miles between stops. To be caught alone and afoot was one of the greatest perils.

I met with the banker and asked about transferring cash. He was quite glad to help with the transaction, but said it would take two or three days for confirmation of funds.

I agreed and gave him the code name, "22 Cal Cole" and the Peterborough Bank. He said to come back Thursday. Stupidly, I had to ask what today was; I had no clue.

"Tuesday." he said. "everyone knows what day it is."

"Apparently not." Was my only reply.

Later I bought another horse. It wasn't near the horse I had, just something they called a mustang. Now several months on the trail, I had some familiarity with horses. The animal was gelded, sound, well-toned with good teeth.

"Now saddle and ride him." I said to the man.

"Ride him?"

"Yes, ride him before I buy him."

"Never heard that one before." But he wanted his money and complied.

"The horse could walk fine and had decent gaits. I bought the animal for forty dollars with a lead halter.

That night I met Houston for dinner. I told him about the second horse.

"Good boy," he said. "Can't go wrong. If that big black I saw you ride in on goes lame at least you won't be afoot. There are other benefits too. If injuns see two horse tracks they will be more wary thinking two men are together. One man is easier prey. Then again, if you are chased, you can drop one horse and they will go after it. Lot easier to chase a horse than go after an armed man. It's all they want anyway, your animals. Nothing else matters to them."

We talked a lot of Indians, the different tribes and where they lived.

The Plains Indians, he said, had been reasonably tamed or killed off. Disease got most, the army took or moved what was left.

"But, travel with caution," he said. "They did not get them all. Still plenty out there on that prairie."

He said that the Comanche down towards Texas were never to be trusted. "Be careful, never camp near your cook fire. Keep your eyes on the horizon. Best to see them first.

"Now farther southwest are the Apache. They are still wild, free and just god damned mean. You get that far, get yourself some riding companions. The Apache will kill you just because. They hate whites and nothing will ever change them."

We had a few more drinks, chatting about the west and what I would need.

"Bullets, have plenty of ammunition," he said. "The injuns are troublesome but it's the white trash out there that are the real danger. They want everything you have and will kill you dead for it. Trust no one west of Kansas City, white or red."

Wednesday was spent procuring necessities for my trip across the prairie. The big purchase was a large double saddle bag for the second horse. I filled it with dried meats, fruits, and other necessities. I purchased additional ammunition as directed.

That night Houston was a no show at the bar, I had just one bourbon and retired.

Thursday morning, I was back at the bank, the transaction had been approved and I got my additional moneys, all in coin. The rest of the day I spent in the library reading papers and noticed nothing unusual. I did note that in a city of strangers, I saw the same man twice, both times he seemed to be watching me, both times once eye contact was made, he vanished.

Thursday night Houston was back in the bar.

"Missed you last night," I said as I took the seat next to him.

"Found me an all-night woman," he said, and it wasn't easy. At my age, the trumpets try to ignore me, but I found one I had used before. She's older but she knows how to ply her trade. She earned every penny and I was glad to give it up. Yes, sir, I was damn glad."

He was laughing.

We ordered a round.

"So, when are you heading west?" he asked.

"First light tomorrow morning." I replied.

"Well, I've gotten what I came to Kansas City for, no reason to dally any longer. Would you like some company? I've not a damn thing else to do and I don't care where we go."

"That would be great," I said and I meant it.

"I'll be ready, my horses and gear are in the stable with yours. Looked over that mustang you bought, nice animal."

I looked up from my drink to see that same man again from earlier in the day. He was standing at the bar, foot on the rail. Two other ruffians sat a table not six foot away. In the door way was a bearded fellow who resembled an older Ralph Gordan.

As I made eye contact with the doorway man, he yelled, "Now!"

Within that split second, six men were hauling iron from their holsters and firing rounds.

My first hit Ralph low left, spinning him around and down. I moved my pistol left and took them as the appeared; one, two, and three, but not before they got rounds off at me.

I was hit twice by whom I did not know, but I got a second round into the man at the bar, then another one into the man at the table. The other man at the table was already down, so, I swung back to Ralph, my hammer fell on a spent chamber.

Houston had gotten rounds off but I had no idea where they went or where his gun had come from. He wore no holster I had seen.

I dropped my revolver and pulled my 22 pistol and was able to put a round into Ralph's ass as he disappeared through the doorway.

As I started after him, I tripped over Houston who was face first on the floor. Two more shots came my way as I fell, both from the darkened doorway, neither hit me. From the floor, still prone, I fired out that 22 into the darkened doorway. I saw no one, I just fired.

Then it was quiet.

I got up and ran to the door, but the street was dark and empty. Ralph had gotten away, but he was hurt, that I knew. I was hurt too, but I wasn't sure where or how bad. Houston was trying to get up, there was a bloody hole in his back.

I rolled him over, blood was covering his chest.

"Damn," he sputtered; blood was coming from his mouth. "I came to Kansas City to get fed and bred, not filled with lead. God almighty boy, you can sure shoot!"

Those were his last words, Hal Houston died right there.

I picked up his pistol and tucked it into my belt. It was a colt.

Chapter 23

▼

The acrid smoke still hung heavy in the room as the bartender peeked over the bar. Two patrons rose from their prone position on the floor. What they saw I did not have a clue as all three went low as the lead flew. At least twenty shots had been fired, maybe more. The nose had been deafening with the confines of the bar.

The resulting carnage laid as they fell, four men were dead and a bleeder had fled. It had been fast and vicious, and I had pain aplenty.

Blood flowed from my left hip just below my belt line. More blood ran from under my left arm, some meat was missing. Even more blood came from my right ear, part of it was also missing.

"Harry," yelled the bartender to a patron, "run for the marshal!" Then to the other patron, "David, you close that front door and keep everyone out until the marshal gets here."

Both men, bug eyed as they were, complied.

"You," he said to me, "load those guns in case he comes back with friends, I'll get some towels for your holes."

A woman came from the inside door, "What happened, Eli?"

"Just one hell of a shootout. Run for the doctor, we got one left standing and hurt bad."

She was gone in a flash, but replaced by another, an older woman with ample girth.

"Hal, my god, Hal!" She said as she ran to Houston. She cradled and cried over him.

Eli helped me with the towels, which we used to cover and press over my injuries.

The marshal and several deputies arrived at the same time as the doctor.

"Jesus Christ, Eli! What the hell happened?" asked the marshal as he surveyed the room. The bartender told it true. He said that Hal and I were hotel guests at our normal table, drinking and talking as we had for several days now. Three men, all strangers, came in. One went to the bar, the other two took that table. They seemed to be watching Hal and I.

"Then a fourth man came in the street side door, looked at this young man here, yelled, 'Now!' and all hell broke loose. Everyone was shooting someone."

"Who shot first?" asked the marshal.

"I don't know," said Eli. "When the man yelled, "now" everyone seemed to have a pistol in hand and I was headed for the floor."

"Who else was in here?"

"David and Harry."

As he was talking, the deputies were checking bodies.

"If they are dead, leave them as they lay." ordered the marshal.

"You, kid," he said to me. "What have you to say?"

"I'm not finished plugging these holes, Marshal." interjected the doctor. "Can't you wait until I'm finished?"

"Marshal," I said, "it was just as Eli reported."

"You shot these three men?"

"I did, and the one that got away."

Just then, a man burst through the street door on the fly. My hand was automatically on the butt of my weapon.

"Marshal! Marshal! Come quick! There's been a shooting on third street! It's bad, really bad."

"How bad? I'm busy here."

"A man and a woman are dead; bullets were flying everywhere. We need you!"

The marshal ordered one deputy to secure the bar and the rest left with him.

As the marshal walked out, he told me to not leave the hotel, that he would be back.

Hurt that I was, there was no leave in me. He did not have to worry. I had lost a lot of blood; my clothes were soaked. What puzzled me, however, was the fact he made no effort to disarm me. Perhaps he saw my handy work and thought discretion was the better part of valor. Or perhaps be believed Eli, that four man had brought to me. Who was to say? I just wanted out of my blood-soaked clothes and to sleep.

Eli and the doctor walked with me to my hotel room, the crying lady followed.

Once in the room, they removed my clothes and the doctor went to work with his medicines, implements, needle and thread.

I looked over at the lady, embarrassed, I guess.

"Rest easy son," she said," I've seen more tally whackers than the master of a boarding school."

When the doctor was finished, he looked at the result of his labors and said, "Fine job, Doctor, just a fine job."

The lady gave her examination and nod of approval.

"Indeed, Orville. Another masterpiece."

"Well, thank you Margret," he replied. "You will need some rest, boy."

The doctor put some dressing on my wounds, commenting that I would have a peculiar looking ear, that he had never seen such a clean piercing. The other holes would be sore, but would heal.

"What's your name, boy?" he aside. "I'll need it for my billing."

"Cal Cole," I said.

"Cal Cole the pugilist from New Hampshire?"

"I'm from New Hampshire."

"No wonder they shot you."

He started for the door, looking at Margret, "What say you about Saturday?"

"Saturday will be perfect." she replied.

Then to me she said, "Now it's to bed with you."

She picked up my gun belt, removed the pistol and sat the chair, revolver in hand.

"I'll be here all night. You sleep. Hal was my favorite. He talked a lot about you; called you his friend. Hal's friend is my friend."

The next sound I heard was that of a crowing rooster. There was pain, but not near the pain I had experienced after my fight with Garrison. This pain was more of a nuisance.

Then I heard the clomping of footfalls coming down the hall. Margret had her head nodded, but she was awake now, standing with that revolver pointed at the door.

There were several large raps to the door then, "Open up, town Marshal."

Margret opened the door and let the marshal in.

"It's early, Charles." she said.

"I know, Margret, but I've a major investigation and I need to talk to Cal Cole."

"You know his name?" she questioned.

"The whole town knows his name and probably everyone for a hundred miles by now.

"Cole," he said, "you are awake, aren't you?"

He was standing over the bed.

"I'm awake."

"Good, I've a long list of questions for you."

He turned to Margret, "Get us some coffee and leave that pistol on the chair."

"Why I'd love to, Charles." By her tone Margret was not pleased, but she left the room.

"Ok, Cole. Start from the beginning and tell it all."

I did just that; I told him the whole story starting with the first fight with the Gordans until the last shot was fired though the doorway into the darkness. I told it all, except for shooting the Gordans in the butt, shooting the foreman, Amelia, Aggie, and a few other odds and ends I deemed not relevant.

"Three of them, you say; John, Ralph, and Richie Gordan are responsible for murder, rape, and robberies from New Hampshire to Kansas?"

"Yes, sir."

"And you have followed them clear out here because they beat you up and buggered your girlfriend five years ago?"

"Yes, and no." I responded. "All I told you did happen, but I was actually on the way to Arizona for business. I just discovered the crimes incidental to my trip."

"You mean you just happened to be following the same trail."

"Yes."

"And one of the Gordans, Ralph, just happened to find you in a bar in Kansas City?"

"Seems so."

At that moment it clicked.

"Marshal, earlier this week, the bank down the street wired my bank in Peterborough, New Hampshire asking for a money transfer. No one knew where I was until that request was made. The next day, the dead man next to the bar started to follow me. I saw him watching me two times during the day then he showed up at the bar with the two at the table. They paid me no never mind until Ralph walked in the door."

"You are saying someone in Peterborough told Ralph Gordan you were in town?"

"Exactly."

"Who?"

"Alice." I said.

Margret returned with three coffees. As we drank, we went over the story again.

"You say you shot them all. What did Hal do?"

"He took a bullet intended for me."

I did not tell the marshal Hal had got off at least two rounds, he for sure hit the number two man at the table. I just did not want to complicate the story, and the Gordans were a vengeful lot. They might come after Margret if they knew there was a relationship.

"Now, Cole, let me tell you what you don't know. A man and woman were shot to rag dolls over on third street about the same time the bar room shooting occurred.

"Witnesses said the couple was walking along the boardwalk and four men stepped out in front of them. The men, without provocation, just emptied their guns into the couple, killing them both on the spot. The shooters ran to their horses and mounted. At that moment, they were joined by a fifth man who had obvious injury to his side. He was trailing blood. All five then rode out of town. I trailed the blood back to the bar downstairs."

"Was there a gal about my age with the couple shot?"

"No," he replied, "just the two of them."

"Was the man missing part of his right hand?"

"Yes, who were they?"

"The Prescotts."

"You know who killed them?"

"The Gordans."

Chapter 24

—————▼—————

Saturday there were six burials at the cemetery. I paid for the three higher up on the hill, the county paid for the three down by the creek. The Prescotts were laid side by side, Hal Houston next to them.

It was just a grave side service; the undertaker, a preacher, the marshal, Margret and myself in attendance. Two grave diggers assisted with the ropes.

Where Jen was, alive or dead, was of great concern.

Afterwards, back at the hotel, I took charge of Hal's effects, all of them. He had a Sharps rifle with ample ammunition, two horses, and his gear. I took his old, greasy, broad-brimmed hat and serape. In his possible bag, I found 74 dollars in coin. His Colt pistol I already had in my belt.

I took my newly acquired mustang and Houston's lesser horse and tack back to the stable and sold it all where I had made the earlier purchase back to the same man for a fair price.

When it was all said and done, Hal had paid for his own funeral as well as the Prescotts. It had been my intention to give the proceeds to Margret, but as I walked towards her place of business, a few doors down from the hotel, I saw her entering arm in arm with the doctor Orville. Naturally I assumed her grief was short lived and that the money's I had paid the Doctor would soon be in her purse.

I pocketed Hal's cash and went my own way.

One more long talk I had with the marshal, re-explaining everything and proving substantially to him that the Gordans were responsible for both my attack and the Prescott murders. He said he had witnesses that affirmed that they talked funny and that the short fat one walked with a limp. He wasn't sure he could prove a case in court, but there was ample evidence for murder warrants for John and Richie Gordan, attempted murder for Ralph. He said those warrants would be issued Monday morning when the court house opened.

Then he asked if and where I could be reached for court.

"Maybe Green Valley, Arizona." I responded. "But I don't think there will even be a trial."

"Didn't think so. Good hunting."

Early Sunday morning I hit the trail west again. I rode the black and tagged along Hal's horse, all his necessities that I wanted were incorporated into my big saddle bags, which that animal carried. That Sharp rifle was lashed to the saddle bags in a manner that allowed for quick retrieval. Hal had plenty of .45 -70 rounds, maybe 100. I stuck six in my holster loops; the rest were on the pack horse.

I had no clue as to Jen, her whereabouts, or condition. All I knew was Dodge City. How or why her parents were in Kansas City without her was a mystery.

Foremost on my mind were the Gordans, one of whom was hurt. He would either need a doctor or grace of God to recover. I strongly felt the latter was not a viable option. He would be looking for a doctor.

Lawrence, Kansas was the closest city of any size. There would probably be a doctor there. It was a full day west. Wary I rode, paralleling the road. Travelling off the road like I chose, added time to my travel. I stopped short of Lawrence and spent the night alongside a no-name stream. The damp travel did little to ease my hip and shoulder pain. A night on the ground helped not a bit either.

Midday I rode into Lawrence witnessing just a huge funeral procession. Everyone in town was either following a hearse or watching.

It wasn't hard to get the lay of it all. Two men came into town, one was wounded, gut shot he was. They went to Doc Belkers for treatment. The doctor did what he could but there was no saving the man. He died right on the doctor's table. The other man went into a rage and shot the doctor dead. Then the man fled west, met up with a gang of others waiting just outside town and headed south.

"Do you have a marshal here?"

"Not now. He is leading a posse after them. They have been gone more than a day now."

"Thanks." I replied. "Is there someone in charge in his absence?"

"Yes, sir. His wife always takes charge when he's away."

"His wife?" I questioned.

"She's a handful. I'd rather meet up with her husband any day."

"Where is the marshal's office?"

I was given directions and made my way to the front door. No one was there, the funeral, I suspected. I took a seat on the porch and waited. Seated as I was, I could see most of the town. At the west end of the main street was a big tree a Cottonwood, I thought. Hanging from a big limb was a man, obviously dead. I wondered who he was and what he did, Lawrence was a no-nonsense town, no doubt about it.

After about an hour, the funeral goers began drifting back. Quite a few disappeared into the different saloons.

A woman, no a huge woman, took notice of me and came to the porch. I wasn't sure I could whip her if I tried.

"Can I help you?" she asked, walking up the step.

"Are you the marshal's wife?"

"I am."

"I have information for your husband in regards to this murder of the doctor."

"How so?"

"It's a long story, but if you have a seat next to me, I'll give it to you. Every iota can be verified by the marshal in Kansas City."

We sat and talked; the lady listened. I gave it to her start to finish, naturally leaving out the not pertinent parts. I told her about the Kansas City shootings and the flight of the Gordans.

Finally, she asked, "What was the name of the man who came to Lawrence for treatment of a gunshot?"

"Ralph Gordan." I responded.

"Ralph Gordan." she repeated.

"Yes,"

"You sure?"

"Yes."

"Well, we didn't catch the murderer of the doctor, not yet anyway. So, at my direction, we hung what we had. Who shot Ralph Gordan?"

"I did."

"And who are you?"

"Cal Cole."

"I thought so, and I suppose you are leaving town to continue your hunt for this Gordan gang?"

"Yes."

"Well, learn to shoot."

"I'll practice."

"Good, if you had been a better shot, we would still have a doctor here and a tree without a dead man hanging in it. Come with me, you can make a positive identification for us.

We walked town to the cottonwood. Ralph's lifeless body hung from the limb either a trophy or warning. I didn't ask. Helga was her name; she had been married to the marshal for more than ten years. He had saved her from her life in a soddy. All that I learned in a walk of 100 yards.

"That's him," I said, "Ralph Gordan. If you need more identification, you can remove his pants. He has two 22 caliber bullet wounds in his ass."

"You put them there?"

"Yes."

"Like I said, you need to practice more."

There were four more hours of daylight and I used them. South, I rode. There was a big city, Topeka, to the west, but there was also a telegraph system. The Gordans were on the run now, and to their thinking, were wanted by name. They would avoid any town with a telegraph line. My guess was south west Texas or maybe Mexico.

Right at dusk, I met up with the returning posse: the marshal led a cavalcade of five men upright in saddles, three other men hung dead over their saddles.

"Woah there!" he hailed.

I pulled up.

"Who are you and your business out here?"

"Cal Cole is my name. I am now four hours south of Lawrence and a long visit with Helga. I gave her my story and identified the man she hung as Ralph Gordan, the brother and cousin of the men you chased."

"Ambush," said the marshal. "They caught us in a crossfire. Three good men are dead, two others are injured."

Then he realized what I had just said.

"She did what?"

"She hung the man that was already dead."

"She hung a dead man?"

"Seems so."

"Good woman."

"Seems so."

The marshal looked over his posse and said, "We need a rest. Four hours home you say?"

"Yes."

"We have no provisions, but a cup of coffee would do us well. Have you any to spare?"

"I do," I said. "There's a creek about ten minutes behind me."

At the creek, we made a fire and heated a pot of coffee. We shared some jerked meat I had. The coffee was served and shared in my two cups.

I told the marshal my story, he told me his.

They had been hot on the trail of four men. Kenny was tracking about as fast as they could ride. They were on open prairie, just grass and saw no one ahead. The track led out onto the point of an arroyo. Four men opened up on them from prone positions, two on the right, two on the left. Three saddles were emptied in the first volley. Two other men were wounded. We skedaddled, waited an hour and went back for our friends."

The ambush location was another three hours ahead. It was now dark and any trail or tracks could not be seen. I chose to stay where I was until morning.

After a couple of hours, the posse mounted and headed north. I slept another night on that hard ground.

Four days I followed tracks south. I found two all-night camps and several stop overs. I was not gaining as I often times lost tracks in the tall grass and had to really search for signs of passage. On the fifth day it rained. On the sixth day, I couldn't find spit. The Gordans had vanished.

Replacing them were five Indians. They were far off, a mile or more, but I had been seen. I cut west towards Wichita; so did they.

Right then, I wished I had practiced shooting that Sharps rifle. There was a bit of high ground to my left, and I made for it. Once atop and over, I found just a bit of shrub to tie off my horses. That Sharp was quick to my hand and five Indians were within a half mile and still coming my way. Their intention was not friendly.

I took a kneeling position, flipped up the open ladder sight and was suddenly perplexed. I had no idea how it worked, and they were closing. I wasn't sure if I had been seen, disregarded the sight, picked out the lead rider, estimated the distance at 250 yards, took dead aim, elevated, touched off a round and killed a horse, its rider spilling onto the ground. My would-be scalpers veered their mounts hard right. I chambered another round from my belt and took aim at another rider, this time accounting for a running horseman. I elevated, fired, and hit another horse, this one in the rump. Both horse and rider went to the ground.

I was on the run to my horses then moving downhill at a gallop. I raced the horses up another rise and over. Again, I tied them off again I found a shooting position, reloaded and waited.

I saw nothing. For an hour, I saw nothing. I decided they had enough, returned to my horses. The Sharps was retied and I mounted the Black. I tugged the tag line and I saw the other horse's ears tip forward. The animal snorted. Exactly where that horse was looking, an Indian, clad in almost nothing was drawing back his bow. He wasn't more than 40 feet away. My Smith was in hand and firing. I probably missed with the first, but not the second.

Another warrior surfaced from the grass even closer and he was running right at me with some sort of ax. At 20 foot, I hit him in dead center with a 44 round. He was down and I was putting the boots to my horse.

Several miles I raced my horses before slowing down. Looking back across that vast grass, I saw no pursuit. It occurred to me that I had shot two horses and only two Indians afoot had attempted to acquire two more. No pleasure did I have. First, I had taken from them their horses, second, I had taken all they would ever have.

This was a hard world out here on the prairie. They would have done the same to me.

Chapter 25

▼

Three days later, mid-morning I rode into Wichita. The sky was literally falling. Rain like I had never seen. The streets were running rivers of mud. Try as I might, I found no available room unless I wished to share a bed.

At a blacksmith shop, I found accommodation for my horses and a place in the loft for myself. There was a smell of manure and flies aplenty, but at least I was dry. The smith, happy for a coin, allowed me to dry my gear over his hearth fire.

I asked the smith, Clayton, was his name, if four riders had recently arrived in town.

"The whole town is full of strangers, cowboys mostly, returning to Texas from cattle drives. They are young, recently paid and drunk. The rain has them trapped here. They are restless and bored. The whores and bars are getting rich."

"You making a few bucks from them?"

"Naw, their horses are not their own, remuda stock mostly, still tied at the rail two days now."

"Where might I get a meal?" I asked.

"The closest is a bar across that river of mud. That's it." He said, pointing to a building on the other side of the street.

"Thanks," I said, "Have you any grain for my horses?"

"I'll see to them. Enjoy your meal if you don't drown getting over there. I've never seen such rain."

My serape and hat were reasonably dry and I put them on. One covered my head, the other my holster. Then with much chagrin, I quickly made my way through the deluge and mud to the saloon. There was a porch that stopped some of the rain. I stomped off as much mud as I could and entered a noisy, dank barroom filled with drunken cowboys. Young they were, all teenagers, maybe 13 to 17, and they were having the time of their lives. Two older men stood the bar, seemly oblivious to the cowboys, locals for sure.

Initially I went unnoticed except for the bartender.

"What will you have?" he asked.

"Coffee and a meal if it is to be had?"

"Yes, sir. Cost you fifty cents cash up front"

"And a place to sit," I said depositing my cash on the bar.

"Not a problem. Follow me."

The bartender led me to a table with two passed-out cowboys flopped over the top. He picked up one and dragged him to the wall and laid him out. Then did the same to the other. Both were small lads, maybe 13 years old.

"They won't mind," said the bartender, "Besides I need a table for a still-paying customer."

Once seated, I soon had a steaming cup of coffee in hand. I drank it and got a refill without asking. The bartender knew his trade.

As I drank, I watched the cowboys waste their money. All were seemly trying to out drink the others. Drunken sots would be an understatement. Periodically a whore came from the back and would yell out, "Next."

"My turn."

"No mine!"

"You have already had three pokes."

They argued back and forth with one of them winning his well-worn prize and disappearing through the door.

The bartender presented a reasonably clean plated covered with a big chunk of steak and fried potatoes. It wasn't the best I ever ate, but I was the hungriest I had ever been. I ate with a purpose.

As I was eating the cowboys began to take notice.

"Where did Howie and Knothead go?" one of them questioned, looking at me and my table.

I continued eating, ignoring them.

"There, on the floor." said another.

"That son of a bitch threw them on the floor. That was their table."

"He don't look so bad."

"Let's show him what happens to someone who messes with Bar B hands," said another.

I continued to eat as about a dozen young cowboys swaggered drunkenly towards my table.

"Hey, boys, I moved your friends." yelled the bartender.

He was ignored and they continued to advance.

I continued to eat as they circled my table.

"Hey, mister. You know what happens when you mess with the Bar B?"

I had one more piece of steak left and I stuck it in my mouth, still ignoring them as best I could. The bartender was now making his way through them.

"Get back, boys!" he yelled. "Let the man be. Get back!"

"I'm finished, thank you." I said. "I'll take my leave."

As I stood up, the oldest and biggest cowboy who was behind me leapt, swung hard with a right hand to my head. I either saw or sensed it coming and moved my head. He caught only the side of my face, a glancing, whack at best.

I came around with my right, caught him square in the face, dropping him where he stood.

Another swung and hit my still-hurting left shoulder. He wasn't near as big as the first. I grabbed him, picked him up like a grain sack, and heaved him into the others, several went to the floor with him.

I was backing my way to the door.

"Leave me alone." I said. "I want no trouble with the Bar B boys. You win."

As I backed out the door, two boys filled the opening, still advancing. Little could I do but land a left to the face of one, a right to the other. Both fell to the floor, blocking passage. I slipped off the porch and disappeared into the rain. My return to the blacksmith shop was via back alleys. I was not seen.

Clayton was not around, but there was wood next to his now waning hearth fire. I stoked it and re-dried my clothing.

The night was spent high and dry in the loft atop some fresh cut hay. My only annoyance was an occasional nocturnal fly and the smell.

"Hey, sleepy head." It was Clayton down below. "Get your ass up and out of here. There must be twenty cowboys out there looking for you. What the hell did you do?"

"I ate a steak." I said, coming down the ladder.

I looked out the door. The sun was up, the sky was blue.

Well-practiced as I was, I had my horses readied and gear packed in but a few minutes.

"Is this the only way out?"

"Yes."

"Well, thanks a lot." I said. "If you'll swing those doors, I'll be out of here.:

"Good luck to you, hombre." He said. "What's your name?"

"Cal Cole."

"Oh, Jesus." he said as I rode out of his shop.

There were cowboys everywhere clomping their horses through the mud. Disorganized they were, spread out up and down the street. I looked left, then right. Fewer cowboys were to the right, I just rode right. As I rode, I was seen and the cowboys began bunching up. I just rode right at them.

There were six or seven ahead, more to the rear who were now moving in fast. Even though most were snot-nosed kids, I was sure each had some type of firearm.

In the group ahead, there were two full grown men, Bar B foreman or owners for sure.

As they blocked my way, I stopped.

"You beat up my boys last night." said one of the men.

"They brought it to me. I had no choice."

"How are you when them come bigger?"

The rest of the cowboys had bunched up behind me.

"If you let me pass, I'll be on my way."

"Hardly." he laughed, "No one messes with Bar B."

"Well, I'm not about to be stomped by Bar B boys, that's for sure."

"I've no intention of stomping you." he said. "I deal in lead."

"And you'll be the first to die." I replied.

"What name do you want on your tomb stone?" he demanded.

I could see in his eyes he had intention.

"Cal Cole." I sneered, and my pistol was out, cocked, and dead on his head.

"Cal Cole?" he repeated and his hands were going up. His counterpart was doing the same.

"Mr. Cole, we are so sorry, so sorry. Boys, drop your pistols, drop them now. Now! You have the road Mr. Cole. I'll tend to the boys; you'll have no more problem from the Bar B.

Chapter 26

▼

Dodge City wasn't much, its hay day had passed. I spent two days there, asking questions about Jen and her possible stay there. What I found out was that I could not even describe her. I only knew her a as a 13-year-old girl. She had to be full grown now, with a different name. She might even be married with kids. I made inquiry also about the Gordans. Nothing was learned except they had some reputation as killers but had not been seen that far west.

As I traveled, I practiced more with the Sharps, leaning how to use the open ladder sight. When I killed an antelope at 500 yards, I knew I had it down pat.

Never did I go hungry as I rode my way southwest. Thirst, however, was becoming an issue. What water I found was utilized. Towns were farther and farther apart. The vastness of the grasslands was an amazement. On and on they went.

Occasionally, I saw Indians, but that Houston horse always spotted them first. His ears pricked and I'd drop my head. Somewhere off on the horizon they would be there. I'd spot them, and wait until they had left.

More often than sightings I would see tracks or come across their camp sites. Wary I rode.

Few were the ranches, a desolate country it was, but when I found one, I was generally welcome. A traveler brought news and different conversation. I could obtain a meal, maybe a bed, and trail information. The location of water holes and streams ahead was essential.

Leaves were turning color as I hit Tucumcari. I'd quit asking about Jen, I saw no point. I would, however, always make inquiry about the Gordan gang. Little did I learn, but it always sparked conversation about outlaws and the men who confronted them, a sort of who shot who.

The most famous pistolero to pass through Tucumcari was years before, some guy named Tyler James. Up north they had a hero named Paxton McAllister. Every saloon had their own outlaws and heroes and they loved to talked about them.

The weather was cold when I rode down the mountain trail into Albuquerque, a big town it was for being in the middle of nowhere. It had been a going concern for hundreds of years. The Spanish then Mexicans, had lived here. I spent a couple of days in a bed and eating Mexican food. Nothing was learned except the local consensus was that if Cal Cole ran into their hero, Jesse Buxton, Cal Cole would be a goner. I'd no desire to meet the man and moved on.

South, I rode along the head waters of the Rio Grande River. It wasn't much of a river; sometimes it had water, sometimes none.

In Socorro, I found mostly Mexicans that were mostly friendly. Some even overly friendly. At a cantina while having a meal, a strikingly beautiful senorita asked in broken English if she might join me at my table. Of course, I agreed and bought her a plate. She was pleasant enough and indeed provoked my primeval thoughts.

I had noticed two sombreroed men at the small bar who were obviously not paying attention. Their lack of interest in this woman was like a big bell going off in my head.

I ate and politely excused myself and walked out. Walking around the corner of the building to my horror I was met by the same two men.

"Senor." one of them said, "you do not have eyes for our sister?"

"Yes, I do." I replied. "A beautiful woman she is."

"You failed to pay her for her company. You have insulted her. We will need payment." He said pulling a pistol from his belt. The other man already had a pistol in hand.

"Give." Was all he said as my shot took him low and hard.

The second man fired and hit only dirt at my feet. My shot took him where he lived. They were both down and I was in the saddle moving.

I headed south, then west on a well-traveled road. I was not followed, but nor would I be welcome again in Socorro.

I had seen this road on a map. It went from Socorro to Payson. Two full inches on the map, but from the incline I was going up, those two inches would probably take two weeks. Within the span of two hours, the temperature went from moderate in Socorro to just damn cold. I knew the first town was Magdalena and I almost missed it. I counted four houses. I passed it by and rode until almost dark, then pulled off the road about a mile further. Back in the buck brush I made a cold camp. No idea did I have whether a posse or perhaps Mexican friends would be in pursuit.

I spent a hard night aground with one tarp below me, my sleeping bag and one tarp over me. My rifle was close to hand. The Houston horse was picketed close. That animal would let me know if anyone was around.

Morning came with a dusting of snow and a sore back. There had been no pursuit, ergo the two I shot were no loss to Socorro.

Two days later I arrived in Pie Town. It was smaller than Magdalena, I counted two houses, one with a sign that said, "Pies."

I knocked the door. It was answered by a most pleasant looking woman.

"I suppose you are hungry."

"I am."

"I suppose you want pie."

"I do."

"Well, come on in. You are my only customer of the day."

I followed her into a kitchen with one large table.

"Sit yourself." she said. "We have elk stew and pie."

"Sounds good to me."

"Coffee?" she asked.

"Please."

The lady didn't talk much. The stew was good, the dried apple pie was better.

"That will be 50 cents."

I gave her the coins.

"Now would you like a place to sleep?"

"I would." I replied and really meant it. The ground was both cold and hard.

"It will be 50 cents. There is a corral in back for your horses. If you hay them, it will be 50 cents."

"Ok."

"It's going to be cold tonight." she said. "If you are in need of a bed warmer it will be 50 cents."

"Ok," I said, not even knowing what a bed warmer was.

"It's getting dark, stable and feed your animals. There is a door from the stable into the back of the house. First door to the right will be yours. I'll light a lamp for you. It's a small room, but your gear will fit along the floor."

"Ok."

Once I had my animals watered and fed, I made my way as directed. The now lamp-lit room was very small but there was a bed and just enough room to stow my rifles and saddle bags, no more. Tired as I was, I just pulled off my clothes, blew out the light, and climbed under the covers. There was no bed warmer but I didn't' care. I was comfortable and asleep almost immediately. I did not even hear the door open. I did not hear the rustling of garment. What I did sense was a warm, naked, body next to mine. Lord help me Jesus, that woman knew how to warm up a bed and keep it warm. It was the best fifty cents I ever spent.

Chapter 27

▼

The ride from Pie Town to Payson was just beautiful as far as the scenery went, mountains, trees and streams. On the tenth day, a majestic Rim appeared to my right. It was the Mogollan, I was sure. I'd met a few travelers, damn few. All were going east. The weather fluctuated drastically from mild in the day to snow at night. It was never deep, just an occasional dusting, but it was always gone by midmorning. I saw elk everywhere, but to shoot one for a meal seemed overkill. I let them be and shot squirrels and what looked like grouse for my meals.

The bad part of the ride was the physical toll it took on my horses. The terrain was either up or down, generally up.

There were a couple of small towns where I took a meal but the cold ground was where I slept.

Twelve days west of Pie Town I rode into Payson. It wasn't much either, just a long line of houses and businesses stretched out for a mile. Only three buildings abutted each to each other. I stopped there and asked direction to the office of David Alan Beam.

"You are here, pal. I'm David Alan Beam and who are you?"

"I was born Calvin Coleman but they call me Cal Cole."

"Cal Cole, the Cal Cole?"

"Calvin Coleman for our purposes."

"Well, come in. I've been waiting for you; sure took your time."

"I had a lot of country to see."

"You rode a horse from New Hampshire?"

"Yes."

"How did you get to Payson?"

"I rode from Socorro."

"That's the long way."

"It was worth it, believe me."

"Good thing you did, I'm afraid you would have been waylaid had you come up from Phoenix. Men have been watching for you.

"Come in, come in. I'll tell you the story."

My horses I tied to the rail.

I got my Remington-Rider, the model one was in my pocket. I took them into the office with me.

"Sit, sit right here." He was pointing to a chair next to a big desk covered in papers. He went to his safe, opened it, and got out a file of papers.

"Here it is," he said," the last will and testament of Robert Russell."

"Was I his only nephew?" I asked.

"Nephew?"

"I knew him as Uncle Bob. I never knew if he had other family."

"Other family?" He questioned, then started laughing.

"Here," he said, "just a second."

Beam opened his desk drawer and pulled out a bottle of bourbon with two glasses.

"Let's have a drink."

"Ok," I said, looking at the bourbon, the first I'd seen since Kansas City.

He poured both glasses and handed one to me, "Cheers." He said, "Here's to Robert Russell." We touched glasses and I took a big swig and just let it rest in my mouth for a few seconds, swished it around a bit more and swallowed. Just that was worth the ride, so I did it again.

"I see you like your bourbon."

"None to be had out on the prairie." I said.

"Damn hard to get up here. I have to order it from Tucson." he chuckled.

"Now, let me read this will your Uncle Bob wrote. 'I Robert Russell, being of sound mind, blah blah blah, do hereby bequeath my Green Valley property, all its assets, as well as all personal property to my only son, Calvin Coleman of Winchester, New Hampshire."

"Son?"

"Yes, sir. Bob told me the entire story about he and Nadine. The man was never your uncle. He was never related to Nadine. He was your father. Glad you brought those weapons for verification. I will record the numbers for legal purposes, but you, son, are the spitting image of your father. There is no mistaking it.

"Want another bourbon?"

"Please."

As I drank, Beam took the weapons and recorded the numbers.

"Wait right here," he said. "I'll need witnesses."

He went out the door and returned with three. Two men and a woman.

"John Keeton, Richard and Mary Marvin," he said, "Cal Cole."

He produced the revolver and rifle and asked each to verify the serial numbers then had them sign what he called an affirmation. They complied and left.

"Oh, they run the general store one side and the assay office on the other. Good people."

For the next hour, Beam laid it all out. Russell owned 50,000 acres in Green Valley. His boundaries blocked access to hundreds of thousands of acres to the east. That property, although valuable, had no access other than to go east without a road for over a hundred miles, and that hundred miles were full of Apaches, namely Geronimo and his tribes.

Beam got out a map and showed me the boundaries.

"Within that 50,000 acres is a sizeable herd of cattle and horses. Mostly mustangs, but Russell introduced a few decent stallions into the herd. There's nice stock back in there, I've seen them. There is lumber too, remember always, trees are money. That timber will probably be the biggest asset to the property. There is also gold and silver. We don't know how much, but he's brought some into the assay office next door. In fact, I've a sack of Russell gold in my safe, that and about $3,000 in cash. It's all here."

Beam got up and opened what appeared to be a closet door. From it, he produced a satchel and rifle. The rifle was a Winchester 73 just like mine. The satchel contained a colt peacemaker with holster and a stack of letters. There was also a framed picture of my mother holding me.

"All the letters are from your mother. The fortune he built was for her. Many times, he told me he was someday going east again for her and his son, but he never got his chance."

"What happened to him?"

"He was bushwhacked, he was found dead in his front yard, one heavy caliber bullet through his chest. He's buried up there by his house."

I poured myself another drink and gave pause to what I thus far learned.

So much to digest. As I sat, Beam moved papers and read. Those letters I wanted to read, but not here, not now.

"Let me ask you, Mr. Beam?"

"Call me David, your dad did."

"Okay, David. How did Bob acquire so much in less than ten years?"

"Let me tell you, the man was driven. He worked from can see to can't seven days a week. He was not afraid of failure, he just kept moving forward."

"There had to be more," I said. "You can't start with nothing and build such wealth in so little time."

"You are right. He did not come to Green Valley with nothing. He had money, a lot of money, when he came in my door. He wanted to invest and I helped him do just that. I knew of an old Spanish Land Grant that could be bought. He had the money and I knew how to do it. We paid the right people to do the right things and made it happen. It's all legal, it's done and as it stands, it's yours. Tomorrow we'll go on a short trip and file the will and transfer paper, we need to sign papers."

"Where?" I asked.

"To Prescott, the territorial capitol, to reassign the deed in your name. This is really a simple legal transfer but there are complications you should be aware of.

"First, there is a party with great interest in your property. In fact, he has men squatting on it right now. I think they periodically steal cattle and horses, but only a few at a time. Bob had his stock branded, horses too. Everyone knows his brand so they are hard to sell. Young stock is, however, easily slipped away. There is no one brave enough to remove the squatters. They are only an attempt to keep the property by right of possession if you fail to sign the deed. Judge gave you one year. We have several months left. Remember, no one knows what you look like, but we are watched, especially the stage line north from Phoenix. They also watch the road to Prescott. I'm sure they lay in wait. They know me by sight, my carriage and horse. But to shoot me does them no good. Any attorney could represent you and copies of everything have already been filed with the court. It's you they want, me too if I happen to be with you. My office is watched. Already it is known a stranger is here."

"They know I'm here?"

"Not for sure. They know someone is here, not who. When we conclude our business, you are to go next door to the assay office, spend some time, then come back here."

"Now?"

"Go ahead, John Keeton is his name. Here, hold out your hand."

I did and Beam placed three nuggets of gold in it.

"Give this to Keeton, he will assay it and record his findings. When you get back, I will have a mine claim for you to file. Then leave, get on your horse and ride somewhere, but be back here after dark. Put your animals in my stable then go up the back stairs to my apartment. Talk to no one. Our ruse is to make them think you are a lucky prospector wanting to file a claim."

"Okay." I said as I left the door for Keeton's.

As directed, I returned to the office then left, got on my horse and rode out of town. In a stand of big pine, I left the road and waited until dark before returning to Beam's. Wary I was now, that pistol was ready.

Once in Beam's apartment I learned that after I left, inquiry had been made with Keeton as to my purpose. Keeton said he acted as sheepish as he could and showed the men, two of them, your assay report. They came into my office demanding my purpose here. As indignantly as I could, I told them a person filing a mining claim is none of their business. They seemed content and left.

We have a plate set aside for you. Eat and go to sleep. Tomorrows a long day."

Chapter 28

I woke to the smell of coffee on the stove. Strange for sure, as for the past many months I woke to all manner of sounds, but not this day. I slept the sleep of the dead.

"Black coffee?" asked Roberta, Beam's wife.

"Please," I said, making my way to the table.

As I sat, David came in the door with a pile of clothing in his arms.

"Everything is ready, all we have to do is eat, change clothes, and you shave."

"Shave?"

"Of course, the whole West knows Cal Cole, the pistolero wears a full beard. Our object is to ride past the men watching the trail to Prescott unchallenged. If you don't go along with my plan we could be shot from ambush and never even see them. Rest assured; they are out there. Now eat and shave. Roberta will help you, she has shears and a razor."

"But-"

"But what boy, I know you think you can shoot your way there but I can't. You are paying me to think for you, so do what I say. This will be much worse for me. When you are done, put these clothes on. We are going to make you look like Richard Marvin."

"And you?"

"Why your wife, Mary, of course and damn you to hell if you let me get killed in a dress."

A half hour later, I was Richard Marvin. David was my cute, fat, wife

Mary. The dress was unbecoming, but the big bonnet was too much. I was laughing and he was cussing.

"What's in it for you?" I asked.

"I may look sweet to you now, but my attorney fee will wipe that smile off your face." I saw him stuff a pistol in his purse.

I holstered up and stuck my other gun in my belt and grabbed my rifle. All of it I concealed under a coat. I thought Richard's hat looked stupid on me and my face felt cold.

The sun was just rising as we headed out to Prescott in the Marvin wagon. As we passed the front of the store, I saw a sign on Marvin's front door.

"Closed, out of town."

"Aren't the Marvin's losing money?"

"No, not a penny. You are paying them to stay closed."

"Can I afford that?"

"Cal, if we pull this off, you will be the richest man in Arizona Territory."

"And you?"

"The second richest man."

"Your fee is that much?"

"Damn straight. I don't wear a dress for free.

"Should we hold hands?" I asked.

"Screw you, Cal."

We laughed and laughed as quietly as we could. Tears were coming from my eyes, his too, his makeup was smearing.

Once out of town, it was all business. That pistol wasn't in his purse anymore. It was under the folds of his dress. My rifle was within easy reach. Our eyes were everywhere.

Logic dictated that any ambush would be far enough from Payson that a rifle report could not be heard. There were small ranches and mining towns along the way. An ambush would not be close to those either. I looked for a desolate spot away from everything, one with cover, one where a wagon and team could be hidden. You might kill Cal Cole and no one would care, but an officer of the court was a different matter. Thought for sure was given to location. Someone had to be always watching the road. That meant more than one man, probably three or four.

Hopefully this silly ruse would work. As we rode along there were thousands of possible locations for an ambush. I watched.

"If we aren't challenged or a least eyeballed somewhere around the East

Verde it will be between Barker's Butte and Camp Verde. That is the most desolate part of the trip." David said. "Thirty miles or so of nothing."

We passed an occasional wagon going the other direction. Everyone waved acknowledgement of passing as people do. One man even yelled out, "Hey Richard, good trail ahead."

I just waved and kept my hat low.

David mostly kept his bonnet low and watched the trail.

That night, we made camp early at the base of Baker's Butte. We found a hidden, secluded place well off the road with a little grass for the horses. His wife had packed us a meal, a little bourbon, two pillows and one heavy blanket.

As we rolled in for the night, I asked David, "You know, I'm new at this. Do I kiss you or do you kiss me?"

"Bite me, Cole."

Long was the night, but at least we were warm.

At dawn we hit the road again for Prescott, still husband and wife. There was no joking now, both of us knew it would be soon. Two miles we traveled, the rising sun to our back, the grade uphill.

From the west we saw a lone rider in the road. He wasn't moving with purpose, just sort of milling about. When he saw the wagon, he nudged his mount forward then veered to his left into a cut between the rocks.

"Wagon coming." I heard him called out.

Back in the trees, I saw camp fire with two men close to it and four horses tied off on a long line.

"Who is it?"

"It's that shop keeper from Payson, Marvin and that butt ugly wife of his." David kept his bonnet tight, but I saw his hand go under his dress.

"Ok," yelled out a man from the fire.

I saw him make the okay sign with his fingers to someone at a higher elevation. Just ahead were two outcroppings, one on each side of the road. I could see a man on each, both held a rifle. We drove the wagon right on past them. They had paid us no never mind.

About a half mile further, I quietly asked Beam how much I was paying him.

"Plenty." He said.

"It's not enough." I responded.

Chapter 29

It was 29 more miles give or take to Camp Verde. Then another 30 or 50 to Prescott. The road, what little there was of one, was miserable. Riding a hard wagon seat made it worse. There were stones everywhere and those wagon wheels seemed to go up then crash down on each and every one of them. Few were missed.

A few miles past the ambush location, we stopped to rest and water the horses. Beam got out of his dress and retrieved his regular clothes from a trunk in the back of the wagon. Mine were in there too and I did the same and felt much better for it, though odiferous I now was.

Beam made the comment too, "Jesus, you smell like you wore those same clothes for months."

"I have, but I feel like myself except for this stubble on my face."

"It'll grow back, give it time," he said. "at least we weren't shot."

"I'll drink to that," I responded.

He produced that bottle of bourbon and we did just that.

For the rest of the day, we talked about my father, his holdings, and his adversaries.

"How did Bob get enough money to build his little empire in less than ten years?" I asked.

"He came with cash, Beam said," A lot of cash. I never knew exactly how much he had, but it was in the thousands."

"Where did he get it?"

"I don't' know, I never asked. But I can honestly tell you he probably didn't acquire it honestly. Most of it he had in a bank in Tucson. When he needed more, he would leave, go to Tucson and return with what was required. Some smaller amounts he kept in my safe."

"You were friends with and helped a dishonest man?"

"Naturally, probably 90 percent of attorney clients are dishonest or they would not need us to defend them. With your dad, I never once saw him do a dishonest act, I would not let him. Everything we did together was legal and above board."

"He paid you fair."

"More than fair. If it wasn't for your dad, I would not have financially survived in Payson. There is no court house, no trials, and hardly any people. Payson is still the wild west, folks handle their problems the old way, fists or bullets."

"Is there any law?"

"Rarely, sometimes a Territorial marshal stops by, but we are located at least 50 miles from anywhere. Were there need of an official, it's a hard, really hard, days ride to even find one, then at least two days back. Marshal's don't kill themselves getting here. What problem there is, is not theirs, and generally resolved when they get here."

Beam again told me about the ranch. He said the main house was stone with a veranda in front. There was a huge horse barn and bunk house for ten men. Another log structure was the ranch kitchen. The place had several wells and good water. One well was inside the stone house, one was inside the ranch kitchen. There was a third drown by the barn. Bob had the wells dug before he built the structures over them.

"He was a planner," Beam said.

"Who did he have problems with?"

"Quite a few over the years. First there were always the Apache. They would come raiding, but Bob and his crew could fort up and wait them out. Many men, both ranchers and mine investors, tried to get his land. He either refused their offers or fought them off."

"Who shot him?"

"No one knows for sure, but everyone suspects Royal Wilkins. He has the biggest outfit in Round Valley to the south. He makes do just fine. Runs several thousand beef and has a few mines dragging up both silver and gold. Wilkens is one of those men who thinks he is always right. I bet he has over twenty men working for him, most gunslingers and outlaw types, who ensure he is. One man has been with him forever, Prairie Pete is his name, maybe the dirtiest meanest bastard ever walked the earth. Folks stay clear of him. You should too."

That night we spent in Camp Verde, still bedding down in the wagon as no rooms were available. We got a meal at the "Everything" house. It was the only business and they did just that, everything. It housed a restaurant, tavern, general store, rooms to let, post office, freight transfers, you name it, they did it.

Bob was called by name and there were apologies for the lack of accommodation.

The next afternoon, we rolled into Prescott and went straight to the Territorial Court House. Beam was known and was given access to the Judge. Apparently, the judge was familiar with the case as after some small table talk, the judge just signed papers as they were presented by David.

"Is that everything?" David asked the judge.

'That's it," he said. Extending his hand to mine. As we shook hands, the judge said, "You, sir, are on track to be the richest man in Arizona, that is if you live long enough."

"Speaking of that," Beam interjected. "have you a will?"

"No."

"Judge, if we could have a few minutes of your time, I'd like to draw up a will for Mr. Cole here."

"Can you do a quick one? I'm about through for the day."

"Ten minutes and I'll be back." We went to the outer room where Beam got paper and pen.

"If you die, Cal, who is all this to go to?"

I thought for a second and said, half to Melba Wisher, Fitzwilliam, New Hampshire the other half to you."

"Are you sure?"

"If I marry and have kids, can it be changed?"

"Yes, of course."

"That's it, for now."

We returned with a written will and the judge signed it.

"Mr. Beam, file your documents with the clerk on your way out."

Chapter 30

▼

Prescott had a fancy hotel, the sign advertised, "Indoor plumbing."

As we entered, I asked Beam what it was.

"They have a water closet at the end of the hall."

"What's a water closet?"

"In indoor shitter."

"Indoors?"

"Yes, haven't you ever seen one?"

"No."

"Well, you will."

We registered and got a room with two beds.

Beam said, "Pay the man, Cal."

I did as directed and received a numbered key for my five dollars.

We were directed to a second floor the room. Once inside, Beam told me to shed those filthy clothes I wore, that he was going for my Marvin outfit. He returned a short time later.

"Put these back on, we will get your trail rags washed."

"Tonight?"

"Yes, they will do just about anything for money."

Over a delicious dinner we talked more.

"About that will, who is Melba Wisher and why did you leave me half?" he asked.

"Well, it was on the spur of the moment and I had to be quick about it. First, I have no known relative and my best friend, Dennis now owns his own profitable business. He would never come to Arizona. I have a good friend in Melba Wisher, she has nothing and never will have being married to a preacher. You have been my only friend in Arizona and saved my life by wearing a dress. You have handled the ranch business for years; you could handle it even better if there was a chance it would be half yours. Now remember this, if you decide to knock me off to get your half early, Melba is the meanest bitch this side of hell itself. She will find you and it won't be pretty."

He went to laughing as did I.

"Two bourbons, please." He asked the waitress. Then we had two more.

When we got back to the room, my clothes were neatly folded over a clean serape.

"How do they get them dry so fast?"

"They have a heated clothes dryer and hot iron. Haven't you been anywhere?"

I've seen 3,000 miles of America and it's all just beautiful."

"I guess you have, but at least for a while you won't smell like a goat."

Morning came way too soon. What I had slept on was pure comfort. The water closet was amazing. All you had to do was finish up and pull a chain, swish it was all gone. Where, I didn't have a clue, but it was just gone.

What I dreaded was that bumpy, bone jarring wagon ride back.

As we were eating breakfast, two men walked in and came to our table. My hand slid down to my pistol; David was extending his.

"John, Fred, glad to see you. Did you get the list?"

"Yes, we did. The wagon is almost loaded and the horses are out front. We just wanted to thank you for the business. We will see you in Payson on Monday."

"Good, good," replied Beam as he pealed out some paper money to them. "This pays for the load; I'll pay your fee on delivery."

They walked away and out the door.

"Who are they?" I asked.

"Teamsters, you don't think we would come all the way to Prescott and not get paid for our travels. The Marvin's had merchandise to be picked up. We drove the wagon up here for them. John and Fred will drive it back full. We will ride their horses home and they will pick them up for the return trip. Everyone wins, everyone makes money and we won't have to endure another wagon ride."

"You think of everything?"

"Everything except how to get past that ambush again."

"Not a worry, David. I've thought about that long and hard."

It was cold when we got to Camp Verde. Colder still when we left in the morning. I knew it took a wagon and team a full day to travel as far as Baker's Butte, the horses would make much better time. As the sun rose, so did the temperature. By mid-morning the day was pleasant, by noon it was Arizona hot again. By my calculations and memory of the trail me were but an hour from things really blazing up.

Curiously, Beam never asked a question about what was to happen, he never said a world.

The grade was downhill and ahead was a dead fall I had previously noted. The ambush spot was less than a hundred yards ahead. When we were close and still out of sight. I pulled up, dismounted and handed the reins to Beam.

"Wait here." I whispered. "Don't come until the firing stops."

"Here?"

"Here." I quietly ordered.

With my rifle in hand, worked my way forward, keeping out of sight. At forty yards I could see a rider in the road, sitting his mount looking east. I could see a man atop one crag but not the other. I eased to the right until I could see him too. The cut where their camp was located was just below him. If nothing had changed, two more men would be lounging the camp. I could smell smoke; they had a campfire still. I checked the area again and made a mental note of where I was going to advance and more importantly, how I would retreat if things went south for me.

Both men on their posts were looking east or dozing, I could not tell. The man on the horse had his head down.

I took careful aim at the man on my left and shot him dead in the back. As he fell, I swung to the man on the right rock who now turned his head my direction, took aim and hit him hard with the next round. The horse man had wheeled towards me, pistol drawn, but useless as he fell from the saddle, dead for sure. That third shot took him where he lived.

Quickly, I advanced to the chosen spot which covered more of the opening to their camp. I heard yelling, then nothing. A few seconds later, two mounted men hit the road east at a gallop. They were putting the spurs to those horses. I was pouring lead into them as they raced. One went down on the first volley, he was hit, but still had spunk as he fired pistol rounds at me. I ignored him, took careful aim at the fifth and squeezed the trigger, topping him from the racing horse.

I'm not sure how many times the fourth man shot at me as he laid prone on the ground, but after I barked his head, he shot no more.

Then there was silence.

After a few minutes, Beam rode up with the horses.

"Jesus Christ, you shot them all." He said.

"Yes, I think so, but we don't know for sure, I can't see back into their camp."

"Didn't you warn them or try to make some kind of deal for passage?"

"No."

"You just up and shot them all."

"They were going to shoot us four days ago, and would have today but we were ready."

"Lord almighty, you just executed five men."

I looked right at Beam, "I can live with it. Can you?"

He was silent.

"When you get home and snuggle in with your wife, it will all go away. This is how I chose to survive. All you have to do is forget and move on. You are alive and those who would kill you are not."

He was still numbed, looking from man to man as they laid dead on the ground.

"Help me get their weapons piled up and retrieve their horses.

"Just do it David."

He did.

I used a horse and the picket line to drag each man to the edge of a cliff a few hundred yards away. The drop was at least fifty feet. I removed from each anything of value, little there was. Then one by one I threw them over.

All their rifles and gun belts were tied to their saddles, then I tagged all five horses. Late was the day as we started south from Baker's Butte with five horses in tow. Long we rode through the night, arriving in Payson well before dawn. Not a soul did we see on the road.

"Cal, I'm an attorney," Beam said, "and a good one, but now I'm an accessory to murder and robbery. I could be hung."

"You will be just fine, just tell no one anything ever, your wife included. We went to Prescot and signed papers, no more. We have developed what I call an unbreakable bond of trust."

I extended my hand and we shook on it.

"Now where is my ranch?"

Chapter 31

▼

The ranch was easy enough to find, even in the dark. "Go east," He said, "until you come to the barbed wire fence. Everything on the other side is yours."

The sun was just breaking as I pulled up to the gate. The sign was dangling down still held by one nail to an overhead cross beam. It read, "R. Russell Cattle Co."

The gate swung easy on the hinges. It had been built well. What I was seeing was a sight to behold. A huge valley of grass, pine mountains to the north and south. Hard it was to believe it was all mine.

I led my remuda through the gate, me on the Black, Hal's horse with my gear and five newly acquired, still-saddled mounts. They were all sound animals. I led the animals to a grove of trees to the south. Each of the five horses was stripped of tack and set free. Their saddles and bridles were left back in the brush for now.

David said the ranch house was a mile past the gate on a northern slope backed up against the Mogollan Rim. As the valley narrowed to less than a quarter mile, the buildings came into view. The house sat higher up than the barn. Strategically it was perfectly positioned for defense of the ranch. A rifle could cover all the buildings as well as travel through the valley. It was a one story, stone structure with a big, covered porch. Six windows covered the two walls I could see. There was a stone chimney at each end. As I neared, I guessed the house to be almost 50 by 30 feet. It was huge.

There was a big barn, 80 by 30 feet built on a stone foundation. It was two stories. The second story was for hay. The corrals and holding pens were extensive and stoutly built.

There were two other wood structures, one was for sure the cook shack, the other appeared to be a bunk house. It could easily sleep a dozen men.

A small brook came from the Rim behind the cabin. It ran to the west of the house. On the knoll beyond was a small cemetery with wood crosses. I guessed that was where my father rested.

As I thought of him, that rage within me began to grow. What he had built was just magnificent, his reward was not the woman he loved sharing it with him, but only a cold lonely grave in the ground nearby.

As I drew closer to the porch, I saw a man dozing in the chair. He must have heard the hoof clomps as he looked up and yelled into the house.

"Rider coming! Rider!"

I was that and kept riding right up to the hitching rail where two already saddled horses nervously moved to the side. I dismounted, tied up, and started up the stairs.

Another man was coming out the door the house in his long johns, a pistol hastily belted on.

"This is private property, stranger. Hit the road back west and lock the gate on your way out." ordered the man in his underwear.

I just kept walking at him and busted him hard as I could right in the nose. He crashed backwards into the house as the porch sitter, now standing, started to draw his pistol.

Mine was in hand and smoking lead before his cleared leather, dead he was before he hit the floor.

I went through the doorway and grabbed the man from the floor and jerked him up. Blood from his nose covered his face. Once I had him up, I ran him to the porch rail and gave him a heave off the porch. He hit hard and did not move.

The dead man I lifted up and carried to one of the horses and threw up him over the saddle.

Again, I addressed the man in his underwear. "You, get up, get up now or I will shoot you too."

He, with some difficulty, managed to stand. Blood now covered his chest. He still had his pistol.

"You can draw that sissy looking little pistol and join your friend, or you can climb up on that horse, take your friend, and go tell Royal Wilkins

116

or whoever employs you that Cal Cole has signed the deed in Prescott, the R. Russell Cattle Company is mine. I'd shoot you too, but then I'd have to dig two holes. I'm tired, I don't give a damn and get the hell off my property."

"Oh, and lock the gate on your way out."

Chapter 32

▼

After Mr. Bloody-nose left with his friend no-more, I went inside the house. A beautiful home it was, but now trashed with whisky bottles and debris. It could take days to clean it out.

What I wanted was some sleep. That and something to eat. The bunk house was a lot cleaner. I thought about sleeping there, but something told me I'd have more trouble yet this day.

I returned to the house and retrieved two rifles left behind by the squatters along with a box of cartridges. I put the horses in the barn and forked them some hay from the loft. I'd need more that's for sure.

Then I grabbed my sleeping bag, some jerked meat from the saddle bag, and my canteen. With three rifles in hand, jerked meat in my pocket, a canteen of water, and my sleeping bag, I made my way over to the cemetery, stopping at my father's grave for but a second.

The marker read, "Robert Russell," no more.

Above the cemetery I found a vantage point that offered concealment, cover and a field of fire. I checked and loaded all three rifles and placed them next to what I picked as my shooting rock. The jerky wasn't great, the water was stale, but the sleeping bag was inviting. I crawled in and slept.

The sun was high when I heard the galloping of horse hooves. They were coming back. I took my position and waited. Nine was the count, nine mounted men and they were coming in fast. They rode straight for the house. They had purpose. Fifty yards out, the firing began. At what I did not know. They were trying to kill a house.

I leveled my rifle at a target, fired and picked another as fast as I could. I fired. Men were down, there was confusion. I just kept picking targets and firing. When that rifle was empty, I picked up another and did the same, then with the third rifle.

I still had rounds left and they were racing back to the gate, four of them and one of those was hurt. I kept firing until the third was empty, then drew my pistol and fired more with no effect except some personal gratification.

In the field in front of me, five men and two horses lay on the ground. One horse was still kicking. I loaded my 73 and finished off the horse, then stuck one more back in the tube. The other two rifles were loaded along with my pistol.

Once loaded and ready, I moved again, this time higher up but on the other side of the house. A new shooting rock was picked and readied. More jerky and stale water was my supper, that sleeping bag was my nights comfort.

I waited again, all night long.

The next day, I had a mess to clean up. Five dead men and two horses. After a breakfast of hot coffee and more jerked meat, I went at my work. To my alarm, there were only four dead men and two horses. One was still alive, but where. I searched long and finally found a spot on the ground with some pooled blood and no body. I tracked what little blood spots I found. Few and far between they were, but the man was headed to an escarpment directly across from the house. Rifle in hand, I began a search eventually finding him sitting upright under a tall pine, dead. The man died with a pistol in his hand and a sneer on his face. I wondered if the man's sneer was for me or those who left him.

Looking around I noticed an oddity, there was a make shift ladder up the escarpment. I climbed it to the top and walked out to the point. From there, I could see the front door of my house 300 yards away. There was of all things an old wood chair and forked shooting stick in the ground in front of it. There were old cigar butts, bourbon bottles and one spent 54-40 casing on the ground.

I sat the chair and leveled my rifle at the house. My 73 would not make the shot, but Hal's rifle would. No doubt did I have, the casing on the ground had held the round that killed my father. The man who fired it liked his comfort, his bourbon, and a good cigar. He also needed a ladder to get up here. He had something else, patience and planning.

Clues I had, planning I needed to do, but there were bodies to move before they started to stink.

I had need of a wagon and team for removal purposes. There were neither on the ranch. I saddled up the Black, stuck my rifle in the scabbard and headed for Payson to rent or borrow them.

I went first to Beams to see if the wagon from Prescott had arrived.

The door to the office was unlocked, I rapped and went in.

"Jesus Christ, the whole town is talking about you. Seems you have killed just about everyone you meet."

"No, no, slow down. It wasn't like that at all.

They brought it to me, came riding in hollering and shooting. I just defended myself as best I could."

"And damn good you are. What is it now? Ten or twelve men dead in just two days."

"Six by my count unless the one that rode off wounded died."

"Weren't there five others"

"Not by my count or yours either."

"Those were all Royal Wilkins riders, all seasoned gun hands and you just wiped them out."

"Like I said, they brought it to me."

"And the squatters?"

"I punched one in the nose, the other drew on me. I had no choice."

"Well, Royal sent for the territorial marshal. Should be here in a few days. He might form up a posse and come for you."

"He might not too. When he gets here, you send him out. He won't need anyone else. I'll tell him exactly what happened out on the ranch. Tell him to ride careful, best to come after dark. I'd bet the farm that someone will try to bushwhack him and frame me.

"Sit down David, calm down. I have information you need to hear."

I told him about the escarpment and the evidence I had found and how it related to my father's murder.

"Dave, I'm looking for a killer, a mean bastard. A man that carries a 54-40 rifle, needs a ladder to climb, who has patience, who can plan, smokes cigars, and likes bourbon."

"You are looking for Prairie Pete."

"Where will I find him?"

"You won't. He'll find you."

"Thanks. By the way, I need a wagon, buy or borrow."

"Ask Marvin, the Teamsters got in earlier, unloaded, and are on their way back to Prescott."

"Did you pay them?"

"Naturally and the Marvins too, out of your cash. You remember the assay report and claim you filed?"

"Sure"

"Prospectors have been flooding in here on the hunt for gold. Watch your property, they will be sneaking around. Gold draws them in like fleas on a dog.

"Son, you ever thought about getting yourself a dog? Something that barks when strangers are coming. Be handy for a man that lives alone."

"No, but it is a thought."

Richard Marvin had no problem renting his team and wagon to me. He said they were still hitched.

"I'll be back with it tonight," I said.

I tied the Black to the back of the wagon and wheeled around onto the road. There was a crowd gathering in front of the local saloon, a place I had not yet visited. It was a fight; no, it was a beat down. Several tuffs had an old Mexican down and they were kicking him. It was not uncommon nor any of my business, but I could not drive on. I pulled up the rig, got down, grabbed one of the kickers and shoved him hard into the other two.

"What did this man do," I demanded, "that he may have needed kicked?"

"He asked for a job," said a bystander.

"Hey, it's none of your business." said the man I had shoved, "Who do you think you are?"

He was coming at me, fist cocked.

It's one thing to cock your fists, it's another to let fly first. I smacked him hard to the jaw and he went back and down, flat on his back and out. He didn't move. The other two stopped dead in their tracks.

"Cal Cole's the name," I said, "and that Mex works for me."

The Mex was getting up.

"I work for you?"

"Sí." I said, not taking my eyes off the other two kickers.

"Cal Cole?" one of them said.

"Yes."

"So sorry, Mr. Cole, we had no idea!"

The Mex was standing next to me.

"Get in the wagon, old man. We have things to do."

"Sí," he responded as he climbed up on the seat. "I work very hard."

I joined him, grabbed the reins and gave the team a flip. We were headed back to the ranch.

"What's your name?" I asked.

"Juan Pedro Rasa Delgado."

"What work can you do?"

"Any that needs done."

"Good, I've plenty to do."

Once back at the ranch and through the gate, I swung the team south to the tree line and loaded up the stashed saddles, tack, and weapons into the wagon. I had Juan drive the team up to the ranch house. I rode the Black, my rifle in hand. It was the escarpment I watched. I saw no movement, nor sign of passage. Still I was unnerved.

As we rode into the ranch yard, I heard Juan remark, "Holy Mother, what have I gotten into? There are dead men everywhere."

"Your first job is to help me clean up this mess. You game?"

"I will not be joining these men?"

"Not by my hand."

"Is there a meal and some coin to be had?"

"Of course."

"I have no place else to go and a debt to be paid. Let's be at it Mr. Cole."

We went to work, Juan kept the pace, did all that was asked and then some. The tack went to the barn, the rifles and pistols to the house. Juan carried them in and came out shaking his head.

"Mr. Cole, a good man you might be, but you live like a pig."

He had spunk.

"Tomorrow we clean the inside. Today we have bodies to move."

First, we used the team and wagon to drag the dead horses out on the tree line. The tack was removed and tossed into the wagon. As we dropped the second one off, Juan asked if I had some beans and chili peppers.

"I'm not sure, but I think I saw some in the house."

He pulled out a knife and slick as a you please, he sliced a back strap off one of the horses.

"This animal has not yet spoiled." He said, tossing a long chunk of meat into the wagon.

We rode back, stowed the tack and Juan took the meat into the house. We removed the holsters and retrieved pistols and a few rifles from the dead. I went through their pockets and found a hand-written voucher on each man. It simply read, "ten free drinks" and was signed, "Royal Wilkins." I put the vouchers where I had found them. A few coins and what nots were recovered, these I gave to Juan.

The bodies were put in the wagon. Then we drove the team over to the escarpment and loaded up the tree sitter. He had the same voucher and a decent pistol. I kept the revolver and left the voucher.

Juan was returned to the ranch house. I tied the Black to the rear of the wagon. The day was late.

"Juan, I will be back long after dark. Find something to do."

Me, my rifle and two pistols, and five dead men left the ranch. It was pitch dark as I drove the team south to Round Valley. I wasn't exactly sure where the Royal Wilkins ranch was, but I knew where it should be, and to my surprise, it was.

He too, had a gate and sign. In the middle of the road just under his gate, I flopped five bodies from the wagon and they were starting to stink. The wagon was returned to the Marvins. The team was put in his holding corral, water was already in the trough, hay was in the manger.

The Black new the way home, all I had to do was open and close the gate.

Chapter 33

▼

The biggest surprise of all was the ranch house and the aroma of something being cooked within. I walked into a lamp-lit, clean home, with dinner on the cook stove.

"Juan, are you married?" I asked jokingly.

"Once," He replied. "Probably never again."

What really surprised me was the array of weapons at each window, rifles and revolvers were laid out for defense.

"You had trouble before." he said, "We are ready if it comes again."

I wasn't sure, but I did not think there would ever be another all-out assault on the house, but what I feared most was Prairie Pete.

I had hot coffee with what he called horse and beans. It wasn't restaurant quality food, it was better.

Sleep was long in coming as I laid on my father's bed. The thoughts I had were not of Bob Russell, not of Jen who I had given up on finding, but rather would the marshal believe me and foremost, Prairie Pete.

In the morning, after consuming what was left of the horse and beans, I had a talk with Juan.

I told him of my father's murder, the escarpment and Prairie Pete.

"I have heard of him." said Juan. "He is a ghost in the night. Even the Apache fear him."

Juan got instruction as to what I wanted him to do. We got an old white-wash basin that had already rusted through. We nailed it to a board. Juan was to go up on top of the escarpment, place it chest high on the chair, give me a signal and get out of the way. I would try and shoot it with Hal's Sharps rifle.

"Senor," he said, "I found something that may help you."

From the dresser drawer Juan produced a small telescope. As I looked the escarpment, it was indeed a help as I could not even spot the chair.

Juan belted on a holster and stuck a revolver in it.

"Just in case I meet a ghost up there." he said, leaving me with the wash basin.

As Juan made his way, I positioned my chair at the window. Then using the sill for a brace, I found I would almost be in position for a braced shot. I needed a few more inches on the sill or a lower chair. Looking around, I found a thick Bible which would work. Out of curiosity, I opened it. The cover page read, "To my love, Bob. May we meet again at Heaven's gate, Love Nadine."

"Damn." I thought out loud. "Damn."

I set the Bible on the sill. The elevation was perfect.

A few minutes later Juan was on the point waving his arms. I saw him clearly in the telescope. I watched him walk back to the basin. I could only see a piece of it. The only real exposure would be a head shot. I took aim, adjusted the ladder sight, readjusted, aimed and squeezed.

Juan appeared and was pointing up. I readjusted and fired again.

Juan appeared and was pointing up. My round was dropping as I was sighted well over the basin.

I lobbed the next one into the pan. Juan came to the point and was waving his arms in an x. I could see the pan had been repositioned so I shot it again. Juan again was waving an x.

I walked outside and waved Juan to come down.

Twenty minutes later, he walked in with the basin. There were two massive holes in it.

"Bueno." he said.

Did you leave everything up there as it was?"

"Sí."

"Good, now we need a distraction, Juan. Yes, something that will cause him to fire. I have to immediately fire back or the ghost will be gone and we will never know where he will set up again. We get one shot."

I set the reloaded Sharps at the sill. It was on a half cock. All I had to do was aim and touch the trigger.

"Now for our distraction."

I began taking off my clothes.

"You wish to shoot him while naked?"

"No, we are going to make a dummy. No, we're going to make two dummies. Shuck your clothes."

We made two dummies and stuffed them with hay. We used grain sacks for heads and Bob's old boots for shoes. Juan's sombrero went to one head, Hal's greasy hat to the other. Mine wore my serape, Juan's just a shirt. We even made a beard for mine out of horse mane. Both had charcoal eyes and mouths.

Juan's Dummy was attached to a pole. Mine we hung under the porch roof so it would swing down and stop when I pulled on a third rope.

The plan was simple. When we thought the time was right, Juan would push his dummy from the back of the house so it could be viewed from the escarpment. That hopefully would cause the ghost's eyes to go left. Then I would pull the rope and Cal Cole would just appear on the porch. Our timing had to be perfect.

If the ghost took the bait and fired, I had but a second to fire back.

We practiced. We could yell back and forth as we would not be heard from 300 yards away.

"Push, pull, fire!"

We had it down pat.

"When will he come?"

"Soon."

Late was the day, Juan prepared another feast, roasted rabbit with gravy over rice.

"Where did you get the rabbits?"

"Out of the two traps I set yesterday. Sí, there were box traps in the barn. I set them yesterday and we have rabbits today."

"How much should I pay you for your labors? You do so much."

"If we survive the ghost, we will discuss it. So far we eat and I am not bored."

It was dark now, but the coffee was hot. I sat the porch in the dark and watched the night. I had no fear of ghosts at the moment. His shot had to be true and he made no mistakes. He might be up there waiting, watching, me watching him.

From the west came a single horse and rider.

"Hello the house!" hailed a voice.

"Come on in." I replied.

The rider drew up at the rail and tied off his mount. Even in the dark I could see he was armed; the rifle was obvious.

"Marshal Maher to see Cal Cole."

"Come up on the porch quickly, then step out of the glow from the door. I fear we are watched."

"Watched?"

"Yes, sir. It's been a problem since I took possession of the property. Quickly now."

"I can't see your face or hands." said the marshal. "Can we go inside?"

"Sure, it makes more sense anyway. Rest easy, I will not harm you, David Beam did give you assurance."

"Yes, he did."

"I want no problem with the law."

Quickly we both stepped in. Juan was sleeping on the divan. I shut the door, then the shutters on the windows before turning up the light.

"Coffee, Marshal?"

"Yes, that would be fine." he said. "Who's that on the couch?"

"That's Juan, my hired man."

"Does he sleep sound?"

"I doubt it, but he will not interfere. He has no stake in this matter."

"I came out here to get your side of this matter. That Royal Wilkins is beyond mad. He says you even dumped the dead bodies of strangers at his gate and he was not going to bury them."

"I'll tell you the story, start to finish."

I did just that, from the banker's office in Peterborough, New Hampshire to his arrival at my porch. The only thing I forgot to tell him was the ambush at Baker's Butte. He now knew about the Gordans, Royal Wilkins, everything.

"That's one hell of a story." he said.

"It's all true."

"And just how did an eastern lad like you learn to fight and shoot?"

"I learned to fight from Derek Garrison's brother. I learned to shoot hunting squirrels with my pistol."

"Derek Garrison, the professional fighter from Boston?"

"Yes."

"He was good, they say, never beaten."

"Oh, he was beaten twice. Once by the man who taught me to box, and once by me when I learned how to box."

"You beat Garrison in the ring?"

"No, sir. In a toe-to-toe on the street in Peterborough."

"Damn, I don't doubt you a bit about fighting or shooting. I've seen the results.

"I believe you, and I believe Royal is behind all this, but I have no prof. He even claims you did in some of his men up near Baker's Butte."

"Does he have proof?"

"No, nothing other than an accusation."

"If he is proven a liar, then he has no credibility. Is that right?"

"Yes, I'd say so."

"Tomorrow go examine the bodies of the men at his gate. Look through their pockets. You will find proof enough within that Royal is an out and out liar. As I told you, I shot them. They worked for him; he can bury them."

"Well, Cole. I need to be heading back."

"Marshal, I want you to stay the night. You need to remain behind these rock walls. If you get shot leaving here, Royal wins as I will be blamed for sure.

"I am going to douse the lamp, then open the windows. We will look and see if we are watched."

"In the dark?"

"Yes."

I blew out the lamp, the house went black. The window I eased open.

"Look way up there on that escarpment. Tell me what you see."

He did. "Nothing."

I handed him my telescope.

"I see a faint glow. A firefly."

"It's winter, there are no fireflies."

"What is it?"

"Prairie Pete, and come sun up he is going to shoot you or me as soon as we leave these stone walls and he don't' care which."

Marshal Maher spent the night in the big chair. I slept the bed.

Chapter 34

▼

Juan had the coffee hot when I woke. He and Maher sat the table talking low. I was sure the marshal was verifying what he could.

I poured a cup and joined them.

"No breakfast, Juan?"

"Not today, we ate it all last night. Besides, if this ghost shoots you what a waste of food it will be."

We had our coffee as the sun rose higher and higher.

"Ready, Juan?"

"Sí."

"Get your dummy. Marshal take a position at the east end window. Just keep back, but I'm sure he won't waste a chancy shot."

First, I walked the house and opened all the shutters. At the back shutter, I saw Juan ready with his dummy.

"Remember, when I yell, 'now.'"

"Sí."

Then I opened the front door.

The marshal just watched.

Next, I took my seat, laid the Sharps atop the Bible. I positioned, sighted, held steady.

"Now!"

I waited a second and pulled the cord. Down came the dummy. Two seconds later, there was a kaboom as a rifle cracked on the escarpment.

My rifle responded before the noise of the first had dissipated. Both reports were almost together.

Then there was silence.

We waited, only a fool goes after a bear before he has bled out. I reloaded the sharps and set it against the sill. As I stood up, I saw the Bible upon which my rifle rested. I thought of my mother who had once held the same book. I've never been particularly religious or superstitious, but right then I knew my shot had been true.

After an hour, I sent Juan for our horses.

"Not a worry, Juan. Shooting you serves no purpose."

Juan came back with the Black and Hal's horse. The three of us then road to the base of the escarpment.

There was a horse tied back in the brush. I climbed up the ladder, pistol in hand and carefully peeked over the top. I saw no one moving, only a body on the ground. As I approached, I had my pistol pointed and ready. Prairie Pete was dead, laying as he sat, the impact of the slug had toppled him and the chair together. One foot still dropped over the front of the chair, his left stuck straight out. He was a weathered, leathery old man, slight of frame and stature. He had worn the garb of another era; mostly tanned leather, hand sewn.

"Best shot I ever saw." said the marshal.

"This old ghost took the head off your dummy at what, 300 yards?"

I just shook my head.

On the ground was another empty bottle of bourbon and half a dozen new cigar butts. I took his rifle and side arm. He had five-hundred dollars in his shirt pocket, the bills now soaked in blood.

The marshal snatched them from my hands. "Evidence," he said. He went through his other pockets and found another chit paper. It said, "all the whisky he can drink in a sitting." It was signed by Royal Wilkins.

"Well, it's not proof for a hanging, but you, Cal Cole, have no worries from the law. I'll deal with Wilkins."

I was walking away, "Hey, Cole. What's to be with this body?"

"You want him?"

"No."

"Well, leave him. He died as he lived. At least he can see the sky."

The marshal and I rode toward the gate. Juan slipped back and snatched the horse.

"You don't need to see me out." Said the marshal.

"I know, but I want to see you safely off the ranch. Remember if something happens to you, I get blamed."

At the gate, the marshal stuck out his hand, still bloody from the money. "You saved my life, Cole. That dead bastard up there was the second-best shot in the whole south west. I'll be in touch."

When I got back to the ranch, Juan was just laughing.

"That Marshal was in such a hurry to collect that blood money for evidence he did not get the real prize."

"What prize?"

"In Prairie Pete's saddle bags was a whole lot more, $1,150, some bacon, coffee, a bit of gold, lots of bullets, some cigars, and lots of watches and jewelry."

Juan dumped the contents onto the table. There was no doubt Prairie Pete was a highway man, an opportunist. A man who hired out.

"It is all yours," Juan said. "You shot him."

"You helped, let's just split it."

That is just what we did. When we were finished, Juan looked just elated. He had more money and foo-frau than he had had in his entire life. He opened up a gold pocket watch in his pile.

"Oh, no." he said. "Oh no, this one is yours. This lady in the watch is the same lady in a picture that is in your second drawer."

It was my mother in the cover of the watch.

All I could think was, what goes around in life, comes around. I put the watch in my pocket.

"Juan, let's go over to the escarpment and take that ladder down."

"I already did."

Chapter 35

━━━━━━━━━▼━━━━━━━━━

For the next two days I rode around the ranch looking at whatever I saw. There were cattle, lots of them. Maybe too many as the grass was short and dry. Lots of horses moved ahead of me, never could I get close enough for a count.

There was wild game, mostly elk, but occasionally deer and antelope.

I saw evidence of mining attempts and a few shacks here and there. Twice I caught prospectors panning the creeks. Those I escorted out the gate.

At the end of those two days, I decided two things. First, I didn't know spit about being a rancher and less about being a miner. What I had was a piece of heaven and I did not have the foggiest of how to manage it.

If I did know what to do, I would need help doing it.

The only things I had accomplished thus far was acquiring the property, defending it, and hiring the best cook in the territory.

We needed to go to Payson. I went to see David Beam, Juan went to Marvin's store for what was needed, I never even asked, didn't care.

Sitting in the chair, I had a hard time even working my dilemma into conversation. Beam rattled on about the shoot outs, bodies dumped at Wilkins gate, the marshal's conclusions, Prairie Pete's demise. On and on he went, and he wasn't even there. He was telling me my own story.

Finally, he settled down and asked what I wanted.

It was then I told him I had no idea what I was doing. These were cattle, way too many; horses, way too many of them too, and at least a half dozen mines started, for what I did not know.

"I'm in over my head, David. Oh, I can keep the property on my own, no problem there. I just don't know what to do with it.

"I have cattle that need to be sold, but I don't know where, for how much, or how to get them where they go. I have thousands of acres of tall trees. I could cut one or two down a day, then what do you do with it? Who saws it up, who do you sell it to? I have potential wealth beyond my dreams, but what would I buy? I already have a beautiful home, horses, food. There is nowhere to spend the money I might acquire to buy what more than I already have. David, I am happiest just shooting folks that want to take what I don't think I want anyway."

"What you need is to pick one thing at a time and work on it. I'd suggest just doing the ranch. You have both cattle and horses. Divide that down to just one, piddle with the others. I would suggest you focus on cattle. We could find a good ranch foreman and some wranglers. You have a bunk house for the crew. We would need to build a foreman quarters. You have cook kitchen. All you need is a cook."

David got his pen out and began writing numbers, adding always to a line, never subtracting.

"Cal, it takes money to make money. How many cows do you think you have?"

"At least a thousand, maybe twice that."

"How many bulls?"

"I don't know."

"Yup, you need help. Let's try it, you came clear from New Hampshire to claim this ranch, at least give it a try."

"What will it cost me?"

"I'm guess five wranglers at fifty dollars a month and a foreman at a hundred dollars."

"That's over $3,000 a year, not counting the house."

"Yes, but if you can sell 800 calves at twenty-five dollars each, that is $20,000 and $17,000 in your pocket, not counting a small house.

"Try it, Cal. The only money you can lose is you never had to begin with. Besides, if you learn the business you can fire the foreman and do it yourself. Now you're at $20,000 a year."

We talked long on the matter. David would advertise for and seek out a ranch manager or foreman. I would hire the wranglers; about five or six.

I left his office still in a quandary. Were in the world could you find cowboys in Arizona? Cattlemen were in Texas and Oklahoma. At least, they normally are. Across the street was that saloon I had never visited, socially, that is.

There were seven or eight horses tied to the rail and quite a hoopla going on within. Inside, I found two factions, miners and young toughs drinking and arguing. I went to the bar and ordered a shot of bourbon. The toughs noticed new meat, namely me, and redirected their verbal assaults at one person as opposed to eight or nine miners.

"Hey, you." one of them said. "This is our party." He was obviously looking to fight someone. "Ya, you." he said as I turned to face him.

As I did, he stopped dead in his tracks.

"Oh my God, no. Not you again. We were just having fun. We are so sorry, Mr. Cole. Don't hit me again."

I wasn't sure, but he looked like the kid from Wichita.

Immediately the toughs straightened up. They went quiet.

"You boys still punching cows?"

"No," he said. "We came up here hunting gold."

"Finding any?"

"Not yet."

"Do you still ride for the brand?"

"Always." he said.

"Want to do it again?"

"If I say no, will you break my nose again?"

"Maybe." I answered.

"I'll ride for your brand any day, Mr. Cole."

"What about the rest of these little hell raisers?"

"They'll ride too."

"Well, follow me. I got plenty of work to do."

Easy as that I rode out of Payson with two mostly grown cowboys and four cowboy wannabes.

Juan eyed the crew as I pulled up at Marvin's.

"Kind of small, aren't they?" He said.

"They won't eat so much. But you better get more food. I'll see you back at the ranch."

On the way back to the ranch, I learned their names. The oldest and biggest was Cleatus, he was eighteen. Thomas was seventeen, almost as tall, but skinny as a rail. The others were all short, skinny, and young. Garrison was fourteen. Benjamin was also fourteen. Donald and Ronald were twins, both claimed to be thirteen, but I had my doubts.

It wasn't much of a crew, but they all had a horse with tack and carried just the sorriest old revolvers in junk holsters. Whatever, they owned was rolled in a blanket tied behind their saddles.

At the gate, Thomas was down and opening it before I gave instruction. When the crew was through, he shut the gate.

Before us was the first field. It was close to a mile square. All the previously acquired horses had herded up and were grazing.

"I need those horses up at the barn corral." I told Cleatus. "They are broke to ride."

"Don, Ron, fetch up that pod of horses out there and follow us." directed Cleatus.

The boys were off at a gallop. As we rode, I marveled at their horsemanship. Within but a few minutes they had all the horses trailing behind us.

The ranch came into view and the crew were noticeably excited.

"We will live here?"

"Wow, how rich are you?"

"Cleatus, I want those horses at the rear of that barn over there."

"Ben and Garry, open the corral gate. Help them herd those horses in." ordered Cleatus. "Is that where you want the horses kept?" he asked me.

"Yes," I answered. "Then have the boys bring in their gear up to the bunk house."

Cleatus was pointing. "Is that the bunk house?"

"Yes."

"Is that a real ranch kitchen there?"

"Yes, it is."

"This is some spread. How far back does your property go?"

"I'm not sure, maybe Kansas."

"Damn."

"Tom, have the boys bring their possibles up to the bunk house after they get their horses settled in."

For the next hour, I showed the crew around. Each picked a bunk and flopped their junk.

Juan returned driving a team and wagon, tail gating his mount.

"Did you borrow the wagon?" I asked.

"Nada, you bought it. If I'm going to cook for all these boys, I will need it for supplies."

"How did you pay for it?"

"Out of my five-hundred and seventy-five dollars. You will pay me back."

"Yes, I will. What about all the stores you have stacked in the back?"

"I opened up a line of credit with the Marvins. You will pay them back. What I don't have is meat for tonight. If you will have some of these boys help me unload, I will be most grateful. Go shoot something."

"Don, Ron, help with the wagon." ordered Cleatus.

I had noticed Thomas was the only one with a long gun, apparently, he knew how to use it as Cleatus told him to go shoot something for dinner. "Gary, go with him."

They went back down to the barn, a few minutes later, they were headed west on their horses. All except Cleatus were helping Juan.

"How is it, they all seem to work but you?"

"Mr. Cole, anyone can work. It takes someone like me to see it gets done."

I had a foreman.

Two hours later, we had elk steaks broiling on the grate.

Chapter 36

▼

For two days, Cleatus and I rode the east range; counting cattle for my tally book, finding the creeks and water holes. The entire trip Cleatus talked cattle. I saw only cows, he saw young cows, old cows, bred cows, bull calves and heifers.

"Way too many bulls out here." He said. "Way too many. At the most, one young bull for twenty cows. These old ones serve no purpose. Most are too old to mount with no semen left to service if they did. Besides, when the poor cow comes in heat, she will be constantly harassed for days. She only needs just one.

"We need to sell them off along with these old rail thin cows. They also serve no purpose. They eat your grass and will give you few calves. If they do, they will have little milk for them. They have to go."

Our estimate was at least 2,000 cattle were back in the valley.

"How long have these animals been unattended?"

"At least one year, maybe longer."

"There are very few steers out here. They are your bread and butter."

"Steers?"

"Yes, castrated bulls."

"Do you castrate?" I asked.

"Sure, the rest of the boys as well. It is part of cowboying. We should also brand the animals, at least the calves as they come. Ear tags with numbers are also helpful if we want to know which calf goes with what cow that came from which bull."

"And why do we need to know that?"

"If you don't keep track, you end up in-breeding your herd. Your end product would be weak, stupid calves. Many will die. As your mortality rate goes up, your profits go down.

As we clear out stock, the grass will improve and the animals will carry more weight. The more weight, the higher your profit."

On and on he went, he was a cornucopia of cattle knowledge.

Finally, I asked, "Just where did you learn all this?"

He looked at me like I was stupid. "I'm from Texas, nothing else to do down there. I've been tending cattle since I could walk. I don't know anything else."

"Family?" I questioned.

"No, they are all dead, my dad in the war, my mother from typhus, sister was snake bit, and a brother trampled in a stampede. I've been on my own since I was ten."

"The other boys?"

"Tom has kin in Tennessee, Gary has a sister somewhere, Ben's parents ran off and left him, Don and Ron don't have a clue to their parentage. They were raised in a San Antonio orphanage. We have all been together for a couple of years now. We are our own family. We hire on different trail drives to survive. Working here is like a dream come true for all of us. We have a roof over our head, our own bed, food to eat, and money to be made. But most importantly, we are still together. We are all we have."

"As you laid it out, we will need additional help to get this head straightened out."

"Yes," Cleatus replied. "At least four or five more hands. Some are needed for the drives; others need to tend stock."

"Where will we find them?"

"Leave it to me." Cleatus said, smiling. "I will get them."

When we got back to the Ranch, David Beam was sitting the porch in my chair. His buggy and horse were tied at the rail.

"Good news and bad, Cal." He said. "The good is I have located a few buyers for your cattle. One is a mine over in Young. They want thirty head every month for slaughter. Man claims to have eighty men working for him. He claims eighty men can easily eat a beef a day. Camp Verde has another outfit that wants twenty a month, the "Everything" thinks they can butcher ten.

"Both of these outfits previously bought from Royal Wilkins but once the marshal made his acquisitions, they are looking elsewhere for beef. There are buyers at the rail head in Tucson, but it is an auction deal. You get what the market will bear. Young and Camp Verde will pay you thirty dollars a head delivered."

"It's a start, David, but there are lots more cattle out there."

"I'll keep looking."

"What's the bad news?"

"No luck on a foreman or ranch manager. Folks want no part of a range war."

"War's mostly over." I said. "Besides, I have filled the position."

"I'd like you to meet Cleatus, the new foreman."

Beam looked Cleatus over as he extended his hand. They shook. Beam looked back at me, never one to mince words, said, "Might young, isn't he?"

"No, he's a man to climb the mountains with. He'll do just fine."

"If you say so."

"I just did."

That night after dinner in the camp kitchen, I sat my porch with my thoughts. David's conversation had brought up several points that needed addressed.

First and foremost, he had mentioned a range war. Many had already died, all Wilkins people. I was fearful the boys could be drawn in, injured or worse. I needed assurance they would not be harmed. Secondly, there was still a score to settle. Wilkins had not shot my father, but he was definitely responsible.

I could just go shoot Royal Wilkins and get it over. That sounded good, but I for sure would be arrested and probably hung. Wilkins had other people do his heavy work. Even with his chits in the pockets of dead men, he was not arrestable. As I thought, it came to me. I didn't even know what he looked like. We had never met. Tomorrow.

Chapter 37

———————▼———————

The gate to Wilkin's ranch stood open. I left it as it was and rode through. It was just a short grade up to the right. As I crested the rise, I could see the log ranch house back along the tree line. Other buildings, all log structures were clustered like a small town below.

Early was the day, the sun just breaking the horizon to the east. A dog lying on the front porch sounded alarm.

I had come calling dressed as Cal Cole. Just a bearded man wearing a dirty, greasy, broad-brimmed hat and a serape, which concealed my revolvers, one holstered, the other in stuck in my belt. The rifle was still in the scabbard.

"Hello, the house." I hailed.

Initially, my only response was the still-barking dog. After a half minute or so, the door opened, and the dog quit barking.

A man stepped out; he wore only a pair of long johns with a hastily belted holster. The pistol was in his hand.

"What do you want?" he demanded, obviously irate at the pre-breakfast calling.

"I'm looking for Royal Wilkins."

"You found him."

Wilkins was a middle-aged man with girth and stature. He was obviously powerful, his underwear strained to hold the bulk within.

"Came to visit."

"Who are you?" he demanded.

"Cal Cole," I said, as I dismounted, keeping the Black between us.

"I came to talk."

I saw him raising his pistol. I was still behind my horse and protected for the moment.

"I said talk, if I wanted anything more, you would have already been shot."

"Well, talk." he replied.

"Most civil conversations begin with an invitation to sit down." I said.

"And most start with an invitation to visit, which you don't have."

"Sorry, but I thought it prudent to have a one on one before others got involved."

"Have a seat, Cole." he said, pointing to a small table on the porch." He still had his pistol in his hand.

"You can put that gun down." I said. "There will be little to gain if you try to shoot me. I would just shoot you back and we both would be dead."

"You that good, are you?"

"I'm here to talk." Was my only response.

We sat at a small table on the porch. He holstered his pistol, but he was not relaxed. Neither was I.

"Wilkins." I said. "I inherited the Robert Russell cattle company from my father. I legally claimed title to the ranch in Prescott. It is mine, all the killings in the world will not change that. I have filed my will with the Arizona Territory. If I'm killed, the ranch goes to my heirs."

He listened.

"Now, I'm not a rancher, I would not make a pimple on a rancher's ass, but I'm learning. If I like it, I'll stay. If I don't, I might sell. You will just have to wait me out."

He offered no comment, but I could see he was getting madder as I talked.

"We have had a few scraps, you and I, over the past few weeks, and your men have suffered for it, but they brought it to me. I did not ask for it. I'm good, damn good at what I can do as you well know. I'm here to tell you face-to-face I want no further problems. We are business rivals, no more. In business it is who can deliver the best product for the most profit, simple as that. Business men like you and I don't need to kill each other. We just out produce, out smart, the other. Actually, both of us can succeed, competition will make us better."

"Is that it?" replied Wilkins.

"I guess so. Oh, one other item. I have hired some boys, all orphans in need of a home. Little guys like we once were. These youngsters remind me of me and how hard it is to start life out without a good home. They are not hired guns they have no stake in this matter. I'm here to tell you if a single one of them is harassed or harmed in any manner, I will kill you just as I killed Prairie Pete. You will never hear the shot that ends your life."

As I stood, Wilkins stood. He was glaring, almost trembling. I knew he wanted to fight or shoot. Uneasy I was as I walked to my horse and mounted.

"Have a good day." Was all I said as I rode away."

That was it, plain and simple. I had drawn a line in the sand, a line only a fool or an idiot would cross. What bothered me most was that hatred could make a man both. There was no more I could do or say. I was done.

Chapter 38

Life at the ranch had fallen into a routine. Everyone had tasks, Cleatus saw to it. A few days after the Wilkin meeting, Cleatus took his leave and returned three days later with five more miniature cowboys. All willing to work for a home. Two were not cowboys, they were assigned to Juan. The other three fell in with the original mix, handy they were with the stock.

Time, I had to myself. Time to read the letters my mother had wrote to my father. As I opened the first, I was apprehensive. I was invading my parent's private world, which was none of my business. What they had was a life of love and secrecy. I chose to leave it as it was. The letter was put back into the envelope, but my eye inadvertently caught only the last line, it said, "I love you, Bob, with all my heart, Nadine."

I put the packet of letters back in the dresser drawer. Someday maybe, someday, I would read them.

One morning after breakfast, I had all the boys report to the ranch house.

"Put all your revolvers and holsters on the table." I said.

You would have thought I'd hit them with a hammer. At first, they were stunned and stone silent, then mad and grumbling as they complied.

The grumbling stopped when I began issuing newer, better, weapons to each. The confiscated weapons of the Wilkin's riders who no longer had use of them was well appreciated. I'd never seen such smiles. Then the entire morning was spent teaching them to shoot. Several were already proficient; more time was spent with those who needed it.

As they lined up, I said, "These guns are to replace the relics you carried.

143

They are tools of last resort. They are not to be played with. If you are caught doing so, I will personally box your ears. I, in good conscious, can not send you out to do a man's job carrying junk for protection. This is a mean world, travel wary. I do not expect trouble for you, but if it ever comes, run first if you can, fight like hell if you can't."

I went down the line making eye contact with each. I wanted them to know I had been talking to him personally.

When I was finished, I said, "Cleatus, put them to work. I need thirty animals to butcher ready for Camp Verde tomorrow."

We were in business.

Beam found us a few more customers, mostly mining camps that wanted ten animals a month to butcher, but three of those camps made a drive of thirty head. We were removing close to one-hundred beefs per month and pocketing twenty-five to thirty-dollars a head. It all added up. After five months, I was easily meeting my payroll and expenses. There were no days off, but my crew was easily entertained in the evenings with horseshoes and checkers. What they loved most were shooting competitions. Most were decent shots, but Tom was good.

Cleatus and Tom, older than the others, would on occasion go to town, the saloon. I thought but more often than not, they came home sober.

Out of the blue, both announced they were getting married to sisters from up in Strawberry, but they did not want to lose their jobs. Not wanting to lose my help, I thought it prudent to build a line of cabins. Over the next several months, we built four identical log cabins in a row on the same elevation as my house, but farther to the east. Two of the newer boys, Nick and Ryan, had a knack for working with wood. They did most of the work.

Once all four were finished, I was pleased with the work. Cleatus took one, Tom took one, and Juan moved into a third. The fourth, we called the guest house.

The wedding was held at the church in Payson. Our entire outfit was in attendance. Great food, great conversation, and of course, decent liquor. A time to remember was had by all except Don and Ron who were either throwing up or falling off their horses on the way home.

The next morning for breakfast, Cleatus and Tom were late, Don and Ron might as well have stayed in bed, both were suffering aplenty, but to their credit, both finished and went to work.

Cleatus finally showed as I was having my last cup of coffee.

"How's being married?" I asked.

He was smiling ear to ear. "Well, I'm late for breakfast, that about covers it."

What a laugh we had.

"Back to my business." I said. "How many animals do we have left to clear off the pastures?"

"Of the old stock, maybe two hundred give or take."

"If we round them all up and make one drive to the railhead in Tucson, will we be able to make monthly deliveries to the mine camps as we have been with our younger stock?"

"Yes, sir, but we need different bulls."

"How many?"

"I'd say fifty."

"Then pick out the fifty best we have left, younger stock, and I'll see if I can trade them for fifty others. Will that do?"

"That would work just fine."

As we talked, Tom joined us at the table. He was smiling too.

"Long night, Tom?" I asked.

"Yes, sir. The longest of my life."

The three of us went to laughing.

Later in the day, I went to see David Beam at his office.

"David, I want you to go see Royal Wilkins. See if he will trade fifty young bulls of his for fifty young bulls of mine. We both need to change out our genetics. If he does, great, arrange a swap of animals. If he says go to hell, get your feelers out to see who will.

"Don't tell him but day after tomorrow, I'm going to take a sizeable head down to the railhead in Tucson. The trade, if he is willing, will be when I get back."

"Ok, but I think his second response is what I will get."

That evening, Beam came out to the ranch.

"Believe it or not, I got both responses from him. The first was an emphatic 'go to hell.' The second, as I was leaving, was more business oriented. He said he would trade after his foreman looked over and approved your stock."

"I will send my foreman over to do the same. Just tell him it will take a few weeks to separate them out. That you will let him know when we are ready."

Beam sat the porch with me as we shared some bourbon.

"Tell me true," he asked. "Did you go to Royal Wilkins' house and threaten to shoot him?"

"Of course, I did. The first time in my life I ever bothered to threaten anyone. Everyone else I just flat shot. If you are going to shoot, don't talk, just shoot.

"I first told him the war was pretty much over and that I had young boys working for me. I simply told him, if one of those boys is hurt, I would find him and kill him, and that's a fact. I will."

"I think he's a believer, but the man hates you. You have what he has always wanted and you bested all his efforts to remove you every time. The talk around town is that his riders refuse to step a foot on the Russell Cattle Company range."

I thought for a bit. "Do you think my dad would mind if we changed the sign?"

"To what?"

"Cal Cole Cattle Company." I said.

"No, I'm sure he won't mind."

"Good, I've been branding my cattle with a double C."

"I'll register the Brand." Said Beam.

"Good, we have been using a bent iron and hitting them twice with it. I'll have the blacksmith in town make me two branding irons, that way we always have one hot. Things will speed up. We are branding cattle every day now."

"How many will you have every year?"

"A thousand, maybe more. Next year I am going to start selling horses too. Plenty of them out there. I'm guessing I've four hundred wandering around."

"Might be a good investment, Cal. Horses sell for a lot more than cattle, and you can't eat them."

"Oh, yes you can. Juan makes a great horse and beans. I'll invite you over."

"Thanks, but no thanks. I'm going home.

"If you are going to Tucson, I want you to stop at the bank. Your father had an account there. I have never known how much money he had. It's yours, you might as well do something with it. I'll wire the bank and tell them you are coming. You'll need a copy of the will and your paperwork from Prescott. I'll have all that ready for you tomorrow.

Chapter 39

▼

This being my first cattle drive, I let Cleatus give directions. I was no more than a bigger cowboy. I rode drag, right flank, wherever I was put. Dusty, hard, bone-jarring work it was. I marveled at Don and Ron. They rode hard, cracked their whips and moved the cattle.

What we had were the bulls we did not want as well as enough old cows to keep their interest. The drive was led by Cleatus and our wagon being driven by Juan. The newly wedded brides were left to do the cooking at home. Tom was to run the ranch.

Cleatus and the boys had ridden north from Phoenix six months prior. They somehow remembered the trail, grass, and watering spots. It was three hard days to Phoenix, then another three to Tucson.

Respect I had for my cowboys. Not one complaint did they make. Everyone seemed to work as a team, with me the weak link.

In Tucson, there was a large cattle pen into which we drove our animals. There were several other herds, but ours was the largest. Our cattle were the poorest. We left home with 258 and logged in 257.

Tucson had several hotels; I picked the best. Myself and eight wore-out, filthy cowboys took five rooms, nine baths, and laundry service. It was late when we got our clothes back, but we were clean as we put them on for dinner. It was the first time my cowboys had ever eaten in a hotel restaurant. They were dead quiet as they were seated at the long table, china, crystal, and silver before them.

The food was excellent, the conversation and tone subdued, the conduct perfect. I could not have been prouder. I paid the bill and was glad to do it.

We slept well past dawn on real beds with clean sheets.

Cleatus and I went back to the yards, the sale was to be at noon. I watched as the animals were moved through a chute, buyers sat both sides. As the animals passed by, the auctioneer took bids. The line of cattle was kept moving. Each buyer apparently had a different color of paint assigned to him, as a man just below the auctioneer upon direction whacked passing cattle with different colors of paint with brushes.

When it was over, we went to the office and waited and waited. Finally, a man came to the counter with our tally sheet. Our 257 animals averaged twenty-one dollars and fifty cents. He gave us a voucher for $5,069.50. They had kept a dollar a head to sell them. We were to take the voucher to the bank for redemption.

Cleatus and I walked down to the bank. There was a saloon across the street.

"I may be here a while as I've other business to do. Why don't you round up Juan and the boys and meet me at the tavern in an hour or two? Then we can get some dinner, get some sleep and head back in the morning."

"Sounds like a plan." he said as he went in search of the crew.

When presented with the voucher, the teller man said, "Oh my. I'll have to talk with the banker. This voucher is unusually large, he has to ok the transaction."

He left then returned with the banker who eyed be over.

"Will you wish this in cash or might you be making a deposit?"

"Probably both." I answered. "First the cash, then I'll consider depositing."

"Good, then you have an account with us."

"I do, the account is under the name Robert Russell, now deceased. I am his heir. My attorney, David Beam was to have wired you about my coming."

"Oh yes, he did and you have the paperwork?"

"I do."

"Well, step into my office."

"I will as soon as I have my voucher redeemed."

"But you may wish to redeposit."

"I might, but put the cash in my hand first. I want to know it's here."

"A peculiar request, but alright. Pay the man, Mitchell."   H   e complied. I put the cash in my pocket and followed the banker into his office.

The banker went into a long dissertation about the account being dormant for over a year and the bank's obligation to oversee the money.

"How much money are we talking?" I was actually growing impatient with him.

"$52,107.37 to be exact."

I was floored, first by the amount, more so as to how my father acquired it.

"With this amount of money, we have to be positive the will is valid and you are who you claim."

I gave him my paper work.

"Ah, yes. But we will have to have correspondence with the Prescott ourselves to validate what you have presented before we can release this amount of money."

"And how long will this take?"

"Several weeks."

"I see." I said, not too happily.

"Explain to me the procedure." He did, but it sounded like legal gibberish to me.

"If I understand this, you are going to send a written letter to Prescott asking the clerk there to validate in writing what you have in front of you. Then you will take that to the court here and have a judge authorize the release of the money, which you don't have on hand. The money will somehow make it's way here and if everything checks out, I can have it."

"Yes," he said.

"Oh, just a few months depending on a court date."

"And I have to ride a hundred miles one way two times before this is over."

"Yes."

"That's four hundred miles through some of the hottest God forsaken snake and Apache infested country there is."

"Yes."

"And the chances of me getting killed increase the banks chances of keeping the money you don't have."

"Yes."

"I'm in the wrong business that's for sure."

"Now, if you'll just sign this request to release information, I can begin the process."

He placed a prepared legal document in front of me. I signed it, "Cal Cole."

He looked at the signature and went ashen.

"Cal Cole, the gun fighter?" He asked.

"Have been from time to time I guess."

"The man who killed near fifty men in the past year?"

"I shot a few that needed it, but not fifty."

"Come back at ten o'clock tomorrow morning, we will have the cash."

"Well, thank you." Was all I said.

He was just glad it wasn't going to be fifty-one.

Chapter 40

▼

The saloon across the street wasn't a particularly nice place, but it had a big veranda outside that offered shade, that and six or seven tables with chairs. Checking inside, I found none of my cowboys, but I did see a few sporting women and a few hang-abouts.

I took a seat under the veranda to wait. A few of the other tables were occupied. Men just idling their afternoon away, they paid me no never mind.

A monster of a man with two others came from the inside. He looked at me then yelled back in, "Customer outside."

A woman, one of the hustlers, came out to my table. She wasn't remarkable in any regard, just a woman plying her trade. She said not a word, just looked at me, as I looked at the monster. He had the mass and arms of Big Ben.

"Bourbon, if you have it. Whisky if you don't."

As she walked by the big man, he grabbed her wrist.

"Hey, your job is to sell your ass, not just the liquor. Now smile and sell it."

He jerked her hand then gave her a shove toward the door of the saloon. "And bring us back three more whiskies.

"Worst whore I ever had here," He said to his two companions.

"Yeah, but under those rags she has a body that won't quit."

"She surely does," added the third.

I had no liking for the three, nor the place, but this is where I had arranged to meet the boys. I would wait. Tucson was a big place; I saw no point to go looking for them. My thoughts had returned to the fortune I had just acquired and what I might do with it.

The woman came back carrying four drinks on a tray. She placed the first three at the big man's table.

"Now, sell that cowboy a poke or you'll answer to me," he ordered. The other two were laughing.

She brought the drink to my table and set it down then abruptly walked away towards the tavern door, well wide of the big man.

"Bitch." He muttered as he got up from his chair and followed her inside.

"Oh well," I told myself. It's a life she chose."

I looked down at my drink. There was something gold beneath it. As I lifted the glass, I could not believe my eyes. I picked up my golden book marker.

"Jen?"

I could hear the big man bellowing inside the tavern, then a slap. I got up and walked inside. Dim was the room; the woman was on the floor looking up at me. The big man was towering above her.

"Calvin?" She said, looking not at him, but at me.

"Jen?"

I reached down and took her hand and pulled her up.

"If you want this worthless bitch, it will cost you five dollars.

Jen was standing now, but the big man wasn't, as I laid him out with a right to his jaw he never saw coming.

The man was strong, I knew it when the punch landed. It was like hitting a tree. He came up fast and was at me like a bull. I side stepped and smashed him hard to the ear as fast as he went by. He was down again, rolled and was back up; blood was coming from both his mouth and ear. It was toe-to-toe, blow for blow. The man could hit, but he could not box and I was cutting him down. For every time I was whacked, I got him two, and my punches were placed to hurt. His nose was smashed and bleeding. One eye was shut and I was working for the other. I moved my feet, it was jab, jab, and punch.

Then I was grabbed from behind. I had a man on each of my arms and the big man was pounding me.

I kicked hard and caught only a thigh in front but it was enough to drive him back a step. But there was no shaking off those who held my arms.

It was then, the cavalry came and piled on. Juan, Cleatus, and the cowboys were doing damage. They had pulled the two off my arms and had them down. Cleatus was smacked hard by the big man, but it was all the distraction I needed, as I stepped in pounding the man hard to his ribs and chest. I was hitting him with all I had.

He was winded, but so was I, yet I kept on hitting. I heard or saw nothing, but a form ahead of me, I just kept pounding his body which did not fall.

Finally, the man went to his knees. He was done, but I wasn't I kicked him dead in his face. He went down and moved no more.

The other two men were also down. My cowboys were standing over them, taunting them to get up.

"Let's go home." I said, gasping for breath.

Jen was cowering over by the bar. I took her hand. "You too. Let's go home, Jen."

Outside the bar, stood our wagons and horses. I put Jen in the wagon with Juan. I grabbed my gold book marker from the table and put it in my pocket.

Cleatus, lead them home. I will catch up with you later. Get as far away from Tucson as you can. I'm pretty sure that big man in there is dead. Juan, look after Jen for me. She's an old friend. I've more business here before I can leave."

I trailed out of town with my outfit, then doubled back, keeping to the back alleys. It was pitch dark by now and I was sure I had not been noticed. The Black was stabled behind the fancy hotel. I entered through the back door and bought another night's stay.

"Where are all the little cowboys?" The clerk asked. "Those were the quietest, most well-behaved young men we ever had stay here."

"They left for home this morning." I lied.

"That will be five dollars." Said the man.

"And with a meal and a bottle of bourbon sent to my room?"

"Twelve dollars." He replied. "And what would you like for dinner?"

"I'm so tired, I don't care. You pick something."

"Yes, sir."

I knew I was a mess, that big man had clobbered me good. The clerk apparently was paid not to notice.

After I cleaned up, had a meal and sipped a fair amount of hotel bourbon, I slept the night.

Straight up ten o'clock I walked into the bank. The bar across the street had a closed sign in the door. The banker was waiting, he had the cash in a bag.

"It's all here, Mr. Cole." He said nervously, handing me a large satchel of money. You'll need to sign for it on this receipt."

I signed.

"Don't you want to count it?"

"Did you count it?"

"I sure did, it's exact down to the last penny. You'll see I left ten dollars in the account to hold it open for you. Hopefully you will do your business with us in the future."

Turning around to leave, three figures stood between me and the door. They all wore badges. They were all armed.

"I've a few questions for you, Cal Cole." said the marshal.

"Can we use your office Gordon?" he asked, but he was headed for the door. The marshal knew the answer.

"Harvey, Harold, guard this door. No one else is to come in. Cole, follow me."

Once inside with the door closed, the marshal told me to have a seat. I did, he sat behind the desk, paying no attention to my signed receipt laying out on top.

"Give it to me straight, Cole." he demanded. "I have talked to all the witnesses so I have a pretty good idea what happened."

I told him exactly what happened. "I brought cattle to the yard to sell, took my tally voucher to the bank, cashed it, then went across the street to wait for my crew. The waitress, Jen, was a friend of mine from New Hampshire that I had been looking for. She had written me from Dodge City almost two years prior. I knew she was in trouble, but I could never find her. She kept changing her name. At the saloon, she recognized me and passed me a gift I had given her when we were thirteen. She was being harassed by that big man as she had not solicited me for favors. They went into the saloon. I heard a slap, went in and saw her on the floor with the big man standing over her. I hit him and the fight was on. We fought, the two men I had seen him talking to came up from behind, grabbed and held me while the big man beat me. Some teenagers came in, pulled the two off me and I finished the fight with the big man. That's the truth."

"Yes, it is." Replied the marshal. "That's exactly the story I got. Did you know you killed him?"

"No, not for certain, but I hit him as hard as I could/"

"That's what everyone said. You just chopped him down like pounding a dull ax on a tree."

"Marshal, it was not my intention to kill him. Oh, I was plenty mad at first when I saw Jen on the floor, but after I hit him once, it was like poking a grizzly with a stick."

"I can imagine. There is not a man in this town, maybe the whole Territory who would go up against Jumbo Miles. Then, on the other hand, everyone wishes they could. Jumbo Miles was a no-good, rotten, son of a bitch. He's run whores and saloons for years, and he was never kind to the women. Your Jen, we called her Lifeless Annie, is just an example. The men out here like and appreciate their whores. They are a necessary evil. We overlook a lot. From what I can tell, you flat beat a man to death, but there is not a jury of your peers that would ever convict you. They want to congratulate you for a job well done.

"My case is filed as self-defense. Now as to your miniature cowboys and the sound thrashing, they gave those other two, good for them, is all I can say. I'd be proud to ride with any of them, teenagers." He was smiling.

"I am."

"There is one more thing you should know. I am positive that about ten years ago, Jumbo Miles and Arizona Bob hit a Wells Fargo cash shipment for close to $150,000. It was their biggest loss ever. We could never prove it. Miles was arrested but later released. No one ever knew Arizona Bob's real name and we never heard from him again. I just found out that Jumbo is wanted in El Paso, Texas for several murders. There is a reward, $1,000. It's yours to collect."

"Marshal, you can collect it for me, then put the money into any civic project you please."

"Why, thank you. I, I mean the town, will be the most appreciative."

Ten minutes later, I was north bound to Payson with over $57,000 in my saddlebags.

Chapter 41

▼

Not being a fool and mostly not trusting the banker, I rode wide of the road to Phoenix. Sometimes as much as a mile. No desire did I have to be waylaid. No problem did I have.

I caught up with the crew just south of Phoenix, then road the wagon with Jen the rest of the trip north.

I tried over and over to initiate conversation, generally, I only got a yes or no. Her eyes were dull, her thoughts were a thousand miles away.

We pulled into the ranch about high noon on the fourth day back. Cleatus got his wife, Jo Anna and Tom's wife, Jo Lynn to come to the house and help me with Jen. She was indeed Lifeless Annie. My instructions were simple, make friends with her, clean her up, and find something clean for her to wear.

The Black and I were headed to Payson.

Beam was in his office when I arrived. "Good trip?"

"Yes, financially we cleared over $5,000 on the cattle."

"Did you inquire about your father's account?"

"I did."

"And."

"It was a sizeable amount."

"And as your attorney, I'm asking what you did with it."

I flopped my saddle bags on the desk. "It's in here. Counting the cattle sales, and deducting our hotel and meals, there should be just over $57,000."

"Jesus Priest, what the hell are you thinking?"

"I'm thinking we can start our own bank. You just sit here all day doing whatever, why not sit in a bank and do both? I want this money invested. We need to make interest on it. If we charged ten percent interest, we could double it in less than seven years."

"We don't have a bank."

"We will build it. I want you to get on this. Buy a lot, hire a contractor. I want it built of stone with two safes, one people see and one under the stone floor beneath your desk. That safe can only be accessed by moving your desk and after hours. We will keep the day to day money in the up right safe people can see and you, David, can loan it out as you see fit to whomever you choose. If they don't pay it back, I will pay them a visit."

"Are you sure?"

"Positive, put what we have in your safe for now. Tell no one, and start tomorrow."

Then I told him the whole story of finding Jen. It took several glasses of bourbon to finish it.

"And she's at your house right now?"

"What else could I do?"

"Walk away."

"Would you walk away from a friend?"

"Never have, but of all the trouble you get into, Cal, you have saddled yourself with a possible lifetime of misery."

"I know, but I don't know what to do. At one time, I would have died for he. She was the love of my life. Maybe she still is. Maybe with time she will become who she was."

"Only time will tell, Cal. Only time."

We put the money in the safe and he gave me the combination.

"You trust me, I trust you." he said.

"Remember, David. The original $57,000 is mine. Whatever we make on this venture is a fifty-fifty split."

"Agreed." he said as we shook hands.

Three weeks later, there was a sign hanging above a twenty-foot by thirty-foot stone building with a partially finished stone floor. The sign said, "First Bank of Payson." Smaller letters underneath read "C. Cole D. Beam proprietors."

That night, after closing Beam and I dug another safe into the ground underneath where his desk was going to sit. We fitted four stones into place over the safe then finished the floor around it. Once the desk was in place, we were both pleased. No one but he and I knew there as $50,000 under his desk. The rest was in the standing safe.

Beam opened up the next day and wrote two short term notes. One for $1,000, one for $1,800. We were to get our money back plus $280. I was a banker, and a rancher; and a depositor as I had an additional thousand dollars in cattle sales to put in the bank.

While this was all going on, I had a ranch to manage and Jen to deal with.

Not much changed. She remained dull eyed and quiet. She slept on the divan I kept my bed. One night, I tried to kiss her, she only cried and went to the divan wanting to be left alone. Jo Ann and Jo Lynn had performed a miracle cleaning her up. Jen was beautiful on the outside, but there was just nothing inside. She was as ever, Lifeless Annie. Frustration was an understatement. Nothing changed for months and months.

The ranch turned a good profit with cattle. Cleatus and the boys were doing a great job. They were making me into a real rancher. I watched and I learned.

Gary was the horseman. He could ride anything with hair. What was an amazement was how be broke wild horses. He would do one a day, every day. He would put one horse in the corral and spend the entire day with it, constantly talking to the animal. Gradually he would have it eating from his hand, then he had his hands on it, brushing and petting it. Next, he would lay a rope on it constantly talking and soothing it. At some point he had a noose over the neck, still talking and stroking. Almost in every case, by mid-day he was leading it with a halter, always calm and soothing the horse his hands always moving. By two o'clock or so, he had a saddle on it still calm in his approach. Then came the bridle, more talking, more hands on. He had sand bags to go over the saddle, adding more weight as he walked the horse around and around. Just before supper, he'd walk the horse between two gates he had set in position. Gary would simply climb up the left gate and step with the stirrups and gradually sit down.

That was it. Calm as you please, he'd ride the horse around the inside of the lot a dozen times. He'd get off, get on, get off, and then open the gate.

As a finale, he would take the horse on a ride to the front gate and back. It was over, he had a saddle broke horse with neither he or the animal hurt.

The math was simple. Gary was getting paid two dollars a day plus board and meals. The horse was worth around a hundred dollars.

One day, while watching him, I asked Garry, "Is it possible to do more than one horse a day?"

"Sure, but why hurry? If I get done too soon, Cleatus will just have me cutting calf nuts."

"Good point." I said. "Keep up the good work."

With Jo Ann and Jo Lynn on board, Juan had more time for other endeavors. He and boys Cleatus could spare built a varmint-proof chicken house. It was huge, maybe twenty-foot by forty-foot. The next time Juan returned from a run to Payson, he had one-hundred chickens. It wasn't long before we had eggs for breakfast and fried chicken on Sundays.

Tom was still the hunter and elk our main stay. I called him the Tennessee ridge runner. That man could track a snake across a flat rock. A dead shot he was.

Life could not be better on the ranch. I simply let everyone do what he did best, what he liked to do, if Cleatus thought it should be done. He was still the foreman.

Everything was working out just fine. Everything but Jen.

Then gradually, she began to take walks, occasionally, even smiling at the crew. Once I saw her wave at Garry as he took another horse to the gate and back. I saw her pick wildflowers and carry them to the house.

Still, she slept the divan and I was a lonely man.

It had become a routine for me, Friday afternoons was a trip to the bank. I would make deposits and check on our investment progress. Almost always we had made money, our average was near a thousand dollars a month. I once asked, "Did we have welchers?"

"Not a one, Cal, they are terrified of you."

I was becoming disappointed in the partnership as I had nothing to do. Nothing except sip bourbon with David on Fridays.

"Now we did make a loan on Monday that has concerned me. Of all people, Royal Wilkins came in and took out a short-term note for $1,500."

"Wilkins?"

"Yes, he said he was low on cash and had a pay roll to meet. He even signed over his whole ranch as collateral. Said he had a big herd being sold down in Tucson as we spoke and the cash would be repaid in ten days."

"Trust him?"" I asked.

"Not a lick, but it's a chance to legally acquire our competition so I took it."

David did have a devious mind, and I liked it.

"Pour me one more, will you, Dave?"

We had another.

As we drank, the door to the bank burst open, it was Don.

"Cal, come quick! Trouble at the ranch. Riders came through and snatched up Jen. They rode off with her."

Don and I were on our horses and headed back at a gallop.

Chapter 42

─────────▼─────────

Cleatus and the cowboys were all armed, saddled, and ready to go as Don and I rode up. No way did I want them to go with me, this was going to be no picnic, men whoever they were, would die. I almost said something, but my boys rode for the brand, they rode for me. I chose to let them ride.

Quickly, Cleatus laid it out. "After you left for town, three men rode through west to east. Jen was alone, picking her wildflowers. Jo Ann from up at our cabin saw them. They had an extra horse. Everyone else was busy and saw nothing. The men grabbed up Jen, put her on the horse, lashed her wrists to the pommel and were gone. They traveled west through our property. Tom is tracking them now."

Jo Ann was standing there with Juan and her sister.

"What did they look like?"

"It was too far away to see their faces. One was big, one was average, and one was short, fat, and walked with a limp."

"Damn," I said. "Gary, switch this black horse out for old Hal."

Gary returned as confused as old Hal. "Why do you want this old horse?"

"Because he's a hunter, let's ride."

Tom left us an easy trail to follow. As he tracked, he broke tree branches straight down. Often times we could see two at a time.

We caught up with him at night fall, he was waiting for us at a gap between two ridges.

"I heard a shot up ahead." He said. "Just a few minutes ago. It was faint, they're still miles ahead of us, but I'm sorry, Cal. I can't see to track. It's just too dark. If we go on, there is a chance we will destroy their tracks with our own horses. It might be days before we could sort it out."

As much as I wanted to go on, Tom's logic made sense. We sat the night where we were, a long, long night. Up ahead, I was sure it was the Gordans who had Jen, but little sense did it make. Why kidnap a woman who personally caused them no grief and take her out into the wilderness, into desolate country? Then it occurred to me. They didn't need her. What the Gordans wanted was me.

I went over and over it. Why was I being lured away? The Gordans could have ambushed me anytime. There was something else.

Daylight came none to quick, but at first light we were on the track again. Tired and hungry we were. An hour later we found a dead horse, it had been shot. The tack had not been removed, but the scabbard had no rifle.

We stood our horses while Tom did a big sweep.

"Three horses continued east, one man walked up that grade," he said, pointing south.

No sooner did he point then a shot rang out from some rocks above. Ben was hit and falling from his saddle.

"There!" yelled a cowboy, "Behind those three rocks!"

I could see the smoke from a fired weapon as could the others. All hell broke lose with the sound of gun fire as twelve different riders emptied their guns into the rocks.

"Take cover!" I yelled.

Before we could even dismount, I saw a rifle stick up in the air, a hat on top of the barrel.

"Tom, Cleatus, go get him."

I went to Ben. He was hit in the side. It looked bad, but as I made closer examination, the bullet had just taken a big chunk of meat.

"Am I going under?" asked Ben, "It hurts so bad."

"You'll be fine, but we have got to get this hole plugged."

Two boys began cutting the sleeves off of their shirts. By the time Tom and Cleatus got back, we had the bleeding stopped.

The man they brought down was also bleeding from just about everywhere. Rock fragments from ricochets was all I could think of as I had never seen a target.

As they walked him up, I remembered him. I stood and punched him right in the face, knocking him to the ground. He was bloody, scared, and I had his attention.

"Now talk. You either tell me everything or I'll give you over to my cowboys and they can do with you as they please."

He looked around. "These are the same little bastards that beat the shit out of me in Tucson."

"And they will do worse this time. You just shot their friend."

"I was just hiding, then I saw the man point right at me. I just wanted to scare you away so I could hoof it out of there."

The ring of boys was closing in and they all had a reloaded pistol in hand.

"Tell it all, leave nothing out, and you'll live to see the marshal. You leave one detail out, I will find you, and kill you. Pretty simple. Talk and the boys won't kill you. Lie to me, and I'll kill you later."

"Ok, I'll tell it true. In Tucson I heard the names Calvin and Jen. You fit the description of Cal Cole. I had two friends in El Paso, John and Richie who had been looking for a Cal and Jen. I rode there and told them, but we had no idea where you went. We worked our way north to Tucson and hung around there waiting for you to come back. We met some wranglers that worked for Royal Wilkins. We learned that Wilkins had no love for you either.

"We rode up to Wilkins' place and talked to him. He offered us $500 each to grab your gal, Jen, and lure you as far east as we could, then kill you.

"The Gordans said they would do it for free, but I pointed out the money would do no harm. So, we hung around while Wilkins went to town for the cash. When we got paid, Wilkins laughed saying it was Cole's own money that paid for his killing.

"The plan was to wait until Friday afternoon, after you left and before the cowboys came in for dinner, make the grab and ride far away to the east. That way, riders would not be associated with him.

"Besides, the whole west knows that the Gordans wanted Cal Cole dead. Wilkins could not be blamed.

"Everything worked well for us until last night. I had need of a tree, when my pants were down, John Gordan grabbed my saddle bag that held my $500, Richie shot my horse. They rode away laughing."

"It all sounds true," I said. "it makes sense, except the part where they shot a perfectly good horse and left you."

"Simple, we are kin, our aunts are sisters. I've been riding with them off and on since we left New Hampshire. Besides, I'm real handy with my gun. One of them would certainly have gotten shot had they tried."

Right then, I realized he talked funny, just like me.

"Who is your mother?"

"Her name is Alice. She works for the bank in Peterborough."

It was all falling together. Alice was telling her son about the Prescott money, which was controlled by the brother. He was helping his cousins.

"What's your name?"

"Bill Busey."

As I looked around, I saw Tom on his horse at the track east. I had to go.

"Cleatus, tie Busey good in his saddle. Never untie him. Let him crap his pants, we don't care. Take him back to the ranch and don't let him get away. Try to keep the boys from killing him. Send someone for the marshal. Keep Busey alive until he gives the law his statement. If he changes what he said here, it's okay to kill him.

"You boys, help Ben into the saddle, one of you ride like hell for the wagon and Juan at the ranch.

"Tom, Gary and I are going on the hunt. The rest of you are needed at home. Wear your guns and ride wary. More trouble may be coming."

"Ron," it was Cleatus taking charge, "you ride for the ranch."

He was giving orders still as Tom, Gary, and I rode east. Tom leading the way, Gary steady breaking branches.

Midday, Tom was off his horse in a flash. He grabbed a sleeping fawn and cut its throat. "I think it's safe to make a quick fire. There's not much meat here, Cal, and we need to eat something. There's a fight up ahead and from the tracks, they are not fleeing. They are leading."

An hour later we were on the hunt again. Three hours later, we found Jen. She was dead on the ground, her dress up over her head. As I pulled the dress down to cover her, the gun in her right hand told the whole story. It was my 22 Cal model one. She had shot herself point blank in the ear.

What horrors she was enduring, what agonies that did and would plague her; she ended by her own doing.

If I could cry, I would have. Gary had no problem filling in for me. Tom just shook his head, then went looking for signs.

I stood there thinking about the thirteen-year-old girl who had stolen my heart, who had given me my first kiss. I thought about how strange life was and how she ended hers with what I was given to defend my own. That gun had been in my dresser drawer. How long had she carried it? Who was to know?

I was feeling loss, pity, and rage all at the same time when Tom walked up with a horse.

"This was the horse she was riding," he said. They must have thought the shot could have been heard, as the two of them lit out of here at a gallop. There is a plateau just beyond the tree line. Nothing out there but sparse grass, rock, and Apache. A rider will have no cover."

"Good." I said, "Then they can't hide. Tom, you and Gary, take her home. Bury her next to my Dad. I'll be back when I finish his."

"You'll need me to track and shoot."

"Tom, I need you to make sure my Jen gets home and buried. What is going to happen will not be pretty, it's not your concern."

He almost argued but the intensity of the rage I felt must have shown in my face.

"Yes, sir." was all he said.

I left Jen in the care of no two better men. A blind man could follow the trail I saw.

Chapter 43

▼

Their trail was easily followed as we were on open ground and they held to a southeastern tract. If I lost tracks over hard ground, I picked it up on the other side.

Things had changed. While they held Jen, they had leverage, they could control any gun battle merely by using her as a pawn. If their plan was to stake her out as bait, it was now for naught.

They knew I was coming for them, and they were running home, El Paso, Busey had said.

As I rode, I began to give Hal his head. As I suspected, he stayed on the trail. The other horses were leaving a scent trail and old Hal was following it.

At one point, he stopped with his ears cocked. There were four Apache, horseback, on the horizon to the southwest. They kept riding; I was not seen.

When I gave Hal his head again, he was right back on the trail. Late afternoon, I crested a rise and saw them, less than a mile ahead.

They had just left what was possibly a tree lined creek. When the Gordans were out of sight, I slipped down to the creek. There was water, just a trickle, but I found a little pool upstream from the horse and drank my fill. On the bank, I saw an empty whisky bottle, I filled it and put it in my saddle bad.

Once quenched, Hal was back on the track; he was picking up his pace. He was gaining.

At the top of a rise, I saw them again, maybe less than a quarter mile coming. They needed to feel fear as Jen did. With my rifle in hand, I dismounted and took a seated shooting position. They were no more than dots in the distance. Wish I did I had my Sharps, but I had my Winchester. It would have to do. I took aim, elevated, and fired.

Where the round hit, I had not a clue, but the two dots had spurred their mounts and were southeast at a gallop.

Hal looked at me like I was stupid as he now had farther to go.

Disgruntled for sure, my horse went back to the track. An hour later, I came up on a three-legged horse. His head was down, the reins dragged the ground. The front right leg was broke.

Two men with one horse ahead, I was gaining. Again, I spotted them ahead, one riding, one walking. Still they were out of range, but I couldn't resist. As before, they were but dots in the distance but I elevated higher and fired.

Both ran, but the man on the horse disappeared leaving the other behind. I advanced. The runner waned fast and he was on open ground with no place to hide or take cover. He had a revolver and used it, trying to keep me away. His shots hit well short. At a hundred yards I shouldered my rifle, took aim and squeezed off a round. The man buckled and fell.

As I rode up, I chambered another and replaced it in the tube with a round from my belt.

It was Richie, and he was gut shot. His revolver was just inches out of reach. He could not move; my shot had apparently hit his spine.

"Help me," he begged, "I'm hit hard, I can't move."

I walked over and picked up his revolver and checked him over for another. He had only one.

'Help me," he was crying now. "I'm dying, I need help."

"Gut shot like you are, your suffering will be long and hard."

"Leave me my revolver."

"So you can ease your own pain like Jen did? Not hardly. I hope it takes days. I hope the buzzards and ants start working on you while you are still alive."

Then came the sneer I remembered, that vicious, sick grin, "You rot in hell Coleman."

"And Richie, you are going to rot right here as you lay."

I rode off after John. Old Hal again on the hunt.

Hal and I followed tracks where I could see them, his nose when I could not for five or six miles. Ahead was another tree-lined ravine and possibly water. Nightfall was setting fast.

I held the horse about a mile from the tree line in just enough of a dip in the terrain to conceal my animal. As we were, I could not see the trees, ergo someone waiting in the trees could not see me. From my saddle bag I retrieved a piece of burnt fawn and my whisky bottle of water. I ate, gnawed, drank and slept most fitfully with the horse reign tied to my left hand, a pistol in my right.

In the pre-dawn, I moved the horse south down in the ravine there were pools of water. Hal was tied off over the top of one of them. I drank from another and refilled my whisky bottle and put it back in the saddle bag. Rifle in hand, I quietly walked up stream searching for an ambusher who might just be watching for me.

About half a mile upstream, I found John. He was on the north bank, prone, rifle at the ready waiting for me. He for sure was not about to be caught out in the open like his brother.

I didn't say a word; I just raised that Winchester. I shot him as he laid. He rolled and squirmed, so I shot him again. He moved no more.

I took his gun belt, revolver, and his rifle. No sense was there to leaving the weapons for the Apache. On his person was nothing at all. In his saddle bags was $1,500 plus a few coins.

I rode his horse down to where I had Hal picketed and changed animals. I put the money in my own saddlebag. Hal was the horse to be on in Apache country.

"Let's go home, Hal." I said, leading the other one.

We headed back the way we came.

Buzzards soaring above led me to Richie.

"Help, help me!" he cried, but only much weaker. His eyes were burnt from the sun. His parched lips were swollen and split.

"Water, I need water."

"I bet you do, Richie." I said as I rode away.

Chapter 44

Three days later, at dawn I rode into my ranch yard from the east. Hungry was an understatement. I went over to the grave yard. Next to my father was a new rock covered grave with a head marker that simply said, "Jen."

There were fresh wild flowers on the grave.

The ranch house was now a vacant lonely place. I went to the ranch kitchen where breakfast was cooking. Juan and the ladies were serving my cowboys who jumped up overjoyed.

"Is it done?" asked Tom.

"It's done."

I ate like there was no tomorrow listening to all the stories being told.

Ben was there, but still heavily bandaged. "Juan, says I'll be just fine, but the scar will last forever."

"I'm sorry." I said.

"Sorry, hell! I can show it to my grandkids. I got this the day I rode with Cal Cole!"

They told about the marshal coming for Bill Busey who wanted nothing more than to be taken into custody.

"He told it true, Cal," said Cleatus, "Just as he laid it out to us. David Beam was here to witness it when he did.

Great breakfast, great reunion it was.

Then Cleatus stood up and gave the day's work list.

"Let's get to work." he ordered.

They were gone, doing whatever he told them to do.

I took a nap in a lonely house. Even though Jen was never a wife and rarely a pleasure, it was a comfort knowing she was here.

Noon I went to see Beam.

"It's never dull on the Double C is it Cole? Glad to have you back. Tell it to me, tell it all."

"You heard most of it from the boys and that Busey fella. The rest is like Baker's Butte. You just don't want to know."

"The Marshal went to get a warrant for the arrest of Wilkins. He wanted you to know that with travel time and the court, it might take him a week to get back. He left three days ago. He said he had enough evidence to arrest but Wilkins had friends in high places; he thought a warrant was prudent. As the marshal left, he said he wished that son of a bitch was just gone when he got back. He did not need a bunch of deputies shot up by Wilkin's gun hands."

"David," I said, "I'm taking a trip back east. I've got friends I want to visit and a few loose ends at another bank to resolve."

"I understand. She was your friend, wasn't she?"

"Maybe more than that.

"David, I want you to manage the ranch while I'm gone."

"Haven't you given me enough to do already?"

"Just the money David. Cleatus will do the rest."

"I will," he said, reaching for our bourbon.

"Not today, but have it ready when I come back."

"Stay in touch."

"Of course."

I left and rode back to the ranch. I got Juan, Tom and Cleatus together.

"I'm taking a trip back east, personal things to do. Cleatus, the ranch is yours to run until I return. Tom, you are his Segundo. Juan, other than cows and horses, the rest is yours."

"When are you leaving?"

"This afternoon. I've a train to catch in Tucson. Have Gary bring up a horse other than the Black and Hal, I'm leaving them here."

I went inside my house and realized what few items I needed. With my revolver belted on and the spare in my belt, I threw the serape over my head. Hal's old hat was on my head. From the corner of the room, I grabbed the Sharps and a handful of rounds. I had $1,500 in cash in my pockets.

There was one last trip to the ranch kitchen for some jerky and a canteen of water.

I said goodbye or waved to those I saw. I spent some time at my little graveyard. I thought about my father and Jen, how they had influenced my life, and how strange it was for both of them to be spending eternity together in a cemetery on a ranch in Arizona. I took the gold book marker from my pocket on wedged it between the boards on Jen's wood cross. As I mounted my horse, I took one last look, then headed to New Hampshire by the way of Round Valley.

Late in the afternoon, I rode my horse past the Wilkins place. I confirmed what I had seen on my prior trip, an escarpment similar to my own, but it was closer to the Wilkins ranch house. The distance was 200 yards or less. I rode south a mile then cut back, well off the road. It was dusk when I hid the horse. It was an easy climb to the top even in the dark. What I noticed first at the top was a dead pine, obviously a lighting strike. Within the trunk was a cavity. I took note of it and was pleased.

At the end of the escarpment, the ranch house was in plain view. The uphill rise from the road did little to block the view one from the other. People like to build houses that had a view from the porch. Never did they realize the view went both ways.

There was a light inside the house. Several times I saw a man go in and out. He sat the porch table and smoked. Then he went in a final time and the light went out. I sat the night watching.

With the morning sun came ranch activity. I saw a man bring a blackened coffee pot to the house and leave. The Sharps I had out tuning the ladder sights to the chair on the porch, chest high. I used a tree branch for support.

Not ten more minutes did I have to wait before Royal Wilkins and his cur dog came out. He was wearing the same long johns and the same gun belt. He had a cup of coffee in his hand this time and took a seat.

I took aim and Wilkins took his last sip of coffee as my Sharps cracked the morning silence. I watched Wilkins fly back in his chair still in his seated position; one leg hanging the chair, the other out straight. He moved no more.

The rifle I stuffed into the lightening split. I worked my way down to the horse and headed to Tucson by way of Young.

Three days later, I was on my first train ride east. I was in what they called first class. I was served meals and bourbon. They even gave me a place to sleep. That iron horse raced east faster than a stallion could gallop.

The wild west I had crossed a few years earlier was no more. Just beautiful scenery and comfort.

Chapter 45

▼

As I peeked in the window, I saw the evening meal being served. Martha was at the stove in her greasy apron. I could hear plates banging in the kitchen. Half a dozen regulars were sitting in their normal spots.

With my hat low, I took a seat by the door.

"What will it be mister? Meat loaf and potatoes or meatloaf and potatoes? That's all that's left, we are about to close."

I just raised an arm in acknowledgement.

"Coffee?" she asked.

I raised my arm again.

I knew the routine, it never changed. The swamper brought the plate of food along with a coffee. Whoever it was, hesitated for a second, then went back to the dish water.

I was smiling inside, she didn't know who I was.

As I ate, the customers now finished left for the night. I noticed most had left a two-cent tip. I had rarely gotten more than a penny, only on the day Derek Garrison beat me up did I get more.

Slowly I ate, sipping the coffee as I did.

The swamper came out and began picking up the dirty dishes. Still I kept my hat low and did not look that direction.

As she was walking back with the plates I said, "Would you ask Martha for a piece of pie?"

The swamper stopped dead in her tracks and turned, dropping the plates to the floor.

"Martha," she said. "Cal Cole wants a piece of pie."

I knew that voice. It was Mell.

"Oh my God," Mell said, "Cal Cole wants a piece of pie."

She had me in a hug before I could stand. She was hugging me on one side, Martha was hugging me on the other. Both were kissing me, both were crying.

"Well for God's sake, Melba, get the man some pie and coffee too for all three of us."

For most of an hour we talked and talked, mostly about what had happened in my absence, which was essentially nothing, but I so enjoyed their voices. Especially Mell's, hers had a soothing tone to it.

Then out of the blue Martha said, "Excuse me." She walked out the front door and started ringing her fire bell. Clang, clang, went the bell. "Cal's home! Cal's home!" She yelled with each clang.

It wasn't five minutes and the whole restaurant was full of old friends. O'Phalon gave me a hug and Big Ben near crushed me to death. Everyone was either shaking my hand, hugging or kissing me. Lots of laughter filled the room. I had no idea I was missed by so many. Mr. Whitaker invited me to come to the bank tomorrow; he had a surprise for me. Martha said she was baking yet another surprise for me. Big Ben said he had one too. People I'd never met were glad to meet me.

After another hour or so the crowd drifted away. I took a coffee to the porch and waited for Martha and Mell to finish up.

When Martha shut the door, I asked if she would like me to walk her home.

"No one has for twenty years, no reason to start now. If you want to walk, walk Melba home."

Martha left going up the hill as she always did.

"If you have a desire to walk me home, I would be appreciative. It's a long walk."

"I went there many times as you remember." I said.

"I have moved," she replied.

We walked and talked. I really didn't care what we talked about. I just loved the sound of her voice. We walked to the last street in town, turned and walked to the end of that street.

She asked me about the west and did I see Indians. She asked about cowboys and the plains.

When we got to the end of that street, we turned again and walked to the end of the next street, just talking.

Then we made yet another right turn and ended up across the street from Martha's. We were at O'Phalon's rear door.

"This is where I lived." I said.

"I live here now. I work for O'Phalon too. What you did, I do."

"And your husband?"

"He ran off years ago with someone prettier and richer."

"He was a fool." I said, "there's no one prettier."

"Did you ever find your Jenny?"

"I did, but she died. It's a long, tragic story, but I'll tell it if you wish."

"Not tonight, Cal, what I want is for you to stay with me, but on one condition."

"What is that?"

"First, kiss me like you love me. I realized the day you rode off to the west that I must have loved you because I cried for a week."

No problem did I have, I held her tight and kissed her like I meant it, because I did, and realized that I always had. What I had seen once and never forgot, was seen again and a whole lot closer.

Low was the glow from the lamp. Soft were the sounds of Mell's sleeping. As I looked around my old room, I saw much had changed. The room had been painted. We slept in a real bed, not my cot. There were rugs on the floor. Pictures of the West hung on the walls, knickknacks, all horses and Indians were placed here and there. Above the bed was a shelf. Stacked on it were as many as a hundred western dime novels. On the bed post hung a holstered revolver. It was obvious the lady sleeping next to me dreamed like I once did of faraway Western places.

As a teenager, I was infatuated with Mell. She was what I thought a lady should be, but she was older and married to another. Age made no difference now, I was happy. I was in love. This is where I wanted to be. I had read once that home is where your heart is. I was home.

But as I looked around the room again, it appeared as if I was going back to Arizona, that is, if she wanted to.

Printed in the United States
By Bookmasters